THE COIN OF CARTHAGE

Bryher: THE COIN OF
CARTHAGE

A Harvest/HBJ Book
A Helen and Kurt Wolff Book

Harcourt Brace Jovanovich, Publishers
San Diego   New York   London

Library of Congress Catalog Card Number: 63-13687
Printed in the United States of America

ISBN 0-15-618407-9   (Harvest/HBJ : pbk.)

B C D E F G H

To the memory of G. A. Henty

FOREWORD

The outline of the war that began in 218 B.C. with Hannibal's march across the Alps and ended with the defeat at Zama in Africa in 202 B.C. is one of the familiar stories of history. Its details, however, are seldom clear even to specialists. The Romans destroyed the Carthaginian libraries when they finally sacked the city or gave them to the Numidians who lost them. They kept only a few agricultural books and these subsequently disappeared. There has been relatively little excavation of the site and much of what has been uncovered was dug up during the nineteenth century when modern techniques were unknown. It is as if England had been defeated in 1940 and we were trying to describe the last hours of London only from enemy accounts.

The struggle was essentially a battle between an emerging barbarian power and an old culture. Carthage, whose empire had been founded upon her control of the sea, lost the fight when the Romans developed new methods of naval warfare. We should not think of the Rome of the Emperors (many people do) when considering the age; the people then were mainly farmers, rooted to the soil and traditional observances. Hannibal's army probably contained few Carthaginians other than officers and the Numidian horse. It consisted of highly trained mercenaries who had no families in Africa to press for their relief or withdrawal.

Hannibal belonged to this present age although it is a point that is overlooked by many historians. The Romans imposed a tribute upon Carthage intended to prevent her economic recovery. Hannibal was able to pay this sum annually from the Treasury without imposing fresh levies, through stopping bribes and preventing the officials from keeping large portions of the taxes for themselves. He also introduced new and intensive methods of agriculture. He must have been as great an administrator as a soldier to have been able to pay the tribute in this manner. His soldiers and the people loved him but the officials whom he had dismissed and the "appeasers" drove him into exile in 195 B.C. He committed suicide rather than fall into Roman hands in 183 B.C.

Knowledge sometimes grows from the strangest seeds. I was nine when my parents gave me *The Young Carthaginian* by G. A. Henty. It fired my imagination because I was just the same age as Hannibal when he had sworn his famous oath to fight Rome. I neither identified myself with him nor with Malchus, the hero of the story, they belonged to the past, but they became my allies. I wanted to be a cabin boy and found that I could reply to tiresome arguments, "if Hannibal was old enough to go on a campaign when he was nine, I am old enough to go to sea."

I was already fond of history but from this moment it became of absorbing interest. I went on to Freeman's *History of Sicily* and the Carthaginian cities in that island when I was twelve and to Flaubert's *Salammbô* when I was sixteen. It was only a step from there to the Loeb Library translations of the Greek and Roman historians and to the vast literature in French and English on the subject, including a study of modern Algeria, in so many ways like ancient Numidia.

I owe much pleasure and, I hope a widening of the mind to the tale that started me roving towards scholarship when I was older. It seems fitting, therefore, to dedicate my own story in turn to the memory of G. A. Henty.

THE COIN OF CARTHAGE

CHAPTER 1

A donkey brayed.

The noise startled a figure huddled on the floor and woke it from an uneasy sleep. "I am Zonas, son of Theodorus, and free born," a voice moaned hoarsely, "your commander promised me protection. . . ." The man came to his full senses, rolled over and struggled to sit up. The place was dark, his arms were bound, he was dazed from a spear butt that had cracked open his head and as he tried desperately to discern something more than the narrow slit of light under a plank, only one fact was clear. He had been flung into a stinking hut where nobody would find him and left there to die. Fortune, whom he worshiped and who had always protected him, had deserted him at the finish.

"My head!" His lips could hardly form the words. Thirst tortured him most and even if a mule train passed outside the hovel where he was lying, what slaves could hear so weak a voice pleading for water? He sank to the ground again and listened. Was that a soldier fumbling at the latch? Perhaps the Numidians were coming back to see if he were dead? He heaved himself over and rolled towards the threshold. It was better to be killed outright than to linger in agony here. Oh, to smell the grass again and to breathe fresh air instead of this sodden mixture of horse dung, mold and his own blood. That one instant would be worth all that he had ever known of happiness.

They had tied his legs together carelessly so that he could move them a little but the ropes round his wrists bit into him as sharply as a small viper had once caught him when he had turned over a stone. The previous days (how far away they seemed) went round and round with the pain as he let his head drop forward on his knees. The Iberian! Oh, why had he ever listened to that thief on a false spring afternoon when the winds were still and the sun had shone for a few hours to trick men into believing that winter was over? "The Carthaginians need bridles," the man had whispered because it was danger-ous to talk about the enemy even in the open fellowship of the waterfront, "the western harbors are solidly for Rome and only a couple of ships got through to Kroton last summer." The fellow had said the words as if he were describing an unimportant incident outside in the street. "They have plenty of gold but not enough leather. What a fortune a man could make if he could take them what they need!"

It had sounded plausible enough in the tavern at Formiae where half the people round him were his neighbors. A Greek captain with a knucklebone on his hand had looked up at him and smiled. Some dice had slipped from a sailor's fingers and a dog had run off with one of them before its owner could stoop to pick it up. He could see the faces now as if they were still round him, a stranger from the hills with five black olives on a saucer, the fair haired Gaul who had once been a slave. "Yes," how lightly he had said that word without a thought of where it was taking him, "but suppose the Numidians catch me on the road, they would take the bridles and clout me on the head." Now it was true. He contracted his shoulders to try to ease the pain in his arms.

"Not with this!" The Iberian had glanced behind him and had then slid a leather tablet towards him, about the size of his palm. "Show this to any soldier you meet and he will take you directly to his commander. You are my friend. We have eaten and drunk together. I will let you have it for a single, silver denarius."

It was not the spiced wine that the rogue had given him. He had actually drunk only one more cup than usual. It was the lamb. He had rejected a sleek, black nosed creature for its leaner, cheaper fellow at the great February feast where all traders sacrificed to Fortune and implored protection for their summer journeys. "Have pity!" he moaned, seeing the impassive figure with the swirling, marble hair that stood inside the temple, "I was not keeping the coins for myself, it was the fodder. The prices rose three times last year." How could he make an offering at all if he could not feed his mules?

"And the savings?" He almost heard a voice speaking to him although it was only a thought tumbling round his aching, troubled head. It was true that he had dug them up from beside the bush where he had buried them, ιo buy ten bridles made in the African manner from the Iberian, the leather token and the name of a village where, as the man had said, "any child will tell you where to go for the sale." He had disregarded the innkeeper's warning although they had been friends since boyhood. "Throw that token away," his friend had said, "it might help you if you were questioned in a town but suppose you meet a Numidian on a lonely path?"

"I will sell him the bridles and come back to Formiae the sooner for you to rob me of my profits," he had joked, he, Zonas, who had known the road and its dangers since he had been no higher than the pack strap on a mule. No, he had angered Fortune, the knowledge smarted as sharply as the cuts on his arms, and she had taken away his wits. "Save me!" he groaned, "and I will offer you the fattest sheep I can buy with the first coins I earn."

The journey had been inauspicious from the start. He had not even told the innkeeper the name of his destination but had joined a group of traders with his servant and two mules and traveled with them towards Frusino until they had come to a narrow valley a week beyond Formiae. He had known he was wrong when he had made a pretext to stay behind, he had felt uneasy walking along the rough track, what should have been fields were a mass of fallen stones. They had found the village after a day's march but when he had followed the Iberian's instructions and said, "I suppose you see a few strangers among these hills?" the headman had looked at him with a blank, almost hostile expression and had not answered. He had sold two cups the following day below their rightful price just for encouragement and he would have returned to the Frusino road the following morning but his best mule had fallen sick, "they must have poisoned it," and he had spent two more idle days drinking atrocious wine and eating the worst bread that he had ever tasted in his life. Even so, he would never have listened to the fellow who had sat down beside him one evening if Fortune had not abandoned him. No, he would have distrusted the man at sight if he had been in his right mind. "I suppose you have no bridles," the stranger had said, "my brother in law in the farm that you can just see up there," he had flung his hand upwards, "is riding to Apulia next week." They had both smiled. At least he had discovered that the region knew that a detachment of the Carthaginian army was there in winter quarters.

The latch rattled. Zonas lifted his head. The door did not move. It was probably the wind. Why had he left his servant behind with the sick mule to follow the stranger alone into the hills without taking one of the precautions that a boy learned before he was a month on the road? He had asked nobody in the village what they knew about the farm, he had taken all the bridles instead of one as a sample, he had hired no guard. It was worse than folly, it was madness but alas, he had cheated over the lamb. "There were the tolls," he moaned, "and the bribe to the guard last year at Minturnae," he struggled violently to free himself in a turmoil of remorse and anger, but his head swam and his wrists began to bleed.

"Where is that farm?" His lips kept forming the words. He remembered that his second mule had stumbled over a long, cracked stone and that was always an omen of bad trading, they had passed the place that he thought the man had shown him and gone higher up the steeper, narrower path, "where is the farm?" He had stopped the

7

mule but the stranger had smiled reassuringly, "just round the corner and my brother in law is waiting with a fowl and better wine than you have had for a week."

The two horsemen must have ridden up behind them at that very moment. He had turned in terror but the guide had greeted them and the men had answered gaily in their own strange language. They were not as dark as he had expected but their faces were cruel. It must have been while he was bending over the pack to get out the bridles that the spear butt had fallen. Had he recovered consciousness for a moment? He seemed to remember laughter and the banging of a door. Since then he had floated in a nightmare of waves, each higher than the other, that had hurled weights of water over his arms and legs as he tried to swim to the surface and breathe. "A sheep," he moaned, coming to his senses for a moment, "I will dedicate the fattest sheep that I can buy if I come out of this hovel alive . . ." but could he, the mules and the bridles had gone and he was as penniless as a ship's boy an hour before sailing time. "Pity me, Fortune . . ." his voice cracked and he sank into a state of half consciousness until something brisk and huge, it was evidently a rat, scurried across his body. He struggled to his knees in disgust, he looked round, the door clattered and this time it opened. "Kill me," he shrieked, trying to raise his fettered arms in supplication, then, as a ray of light fell across the threshold, he found himself staring into the brown, liquid eyes of a thin, undersized donkey.

"Welcome! Hermes has sent you." An unexpected meeting with an ass was the luckiest thing that could happen to a trader. The sun was beating on the grass, it was noon and as he half rolled and half crawled outside, he judged that he must have been almost two days inside the stable. He tried to look round. There was a small building surrounded by a wall a little distance away. There would be a well if that was the farm but how could he reach it with the hobbles round his legs and yet he would have to try. Otherwise the cold mountain night would finish what the spear butt had begun. Perhaps someone would find him? He opened his mouth but all the sound that he could manage was a groan. His head flopped onto the ground. Supposing the Numidians were still there? He could almost taste the sick, black terror that surged across his body at the thought but at least his wits were coming back to him now that he was in the open air.

What had he shouted so often to his companions over the wine? "Take experience as it comes. If the market's bad there may be a fortunate bargain at the next town and if the Messenger taps you on the shoulder follow him without grumbling, it is still the road." He had been summoned but perhaps from shame, every fiber in him was struggling to live while he lay, tied up and helpless like a terrified, about to be slaughtered beast, and it was due to his own stupidity and his neglect of the proper February rites.

The donkey, disappointed at finding no fodder in the stall, nudged him gently. He could feel the beast's soft muzzle but his mind was drifting again until he was dreaming hazily of his mother's kitchen. Once, when he had been barely tall enough to look over the rim, he had dipped his head suddenly into the fountain that had stood outside the door. The water had splashed into his eyes and taken his breath away and it had seemed colder that hot day than the snow that he had stepped into once, but only once, on a mountain path. Water, if he could struggle to the farm even the Numidians might give him one drink before they killed him. He rolled over with a tremendous effort, the sweat poured down his back and then he realized that he was more of a prisoner than ever. The looser of the two ropes had tangled and he could not even crawl.

"Sikelia!" It was a whisper rather than a voice. A small boy's head peered round the hut, he was looking for the donkey. "Help me!" Zonas begged, holding out his roped hands as far as he was able, "help in the name of Hermes, help!" He tried to sit up but the terrified urchin bolted. There was only one hope; the child might have gone to fetch his father. How ugly and desolate a place it was. A discolored bone, left by some dog, stuck out of a heap of nettles and a length away, a clump of field flowers had been torn from the ground and lay with its roots in the air and the leaves withering in the dust. Zonas closed his eyes, knowing that it was here that he had to die unless the boy came back.

"Was it the Numidians?" a voice asked.

The child was standing several paces away, looking at Zonas with an anxious face. There was a patch at one side of his short, rough tunic and he had a herder's knife in his hand.

"Help me!" the trader groaned, "I am Zonas, son of Theodorus, and I left servants in the valley. Take me to them and I will give you half of what I have."

The boy came nearer. He poured a little water from a leather bottle into the trader's mouth and began to hack at the rope that bound his legs. "How long have you been here?" he asked.

"Two days. It was the Numidians. They knocked me down, robbed me and flung me into that hut."

"How did you get out?"

"It was your donkey, she lifted the latch."

"Yes," the boy nodded as if relieved by the information, "it is a trick she has learned. She liked being with the ox and is still looking for it."

"And your parents?" Zonas felt a sudden anxiety racing through him again, "are the Numidians at the farm?"

"I do not know. My name is Bassus and I am living with my grandparents." The rope dropped from the trader's ankles but the legs were so stiff that he could not straighten them and the boy began to rub them with strong, rough fingers. "My mother died from a fever when I was a baby and they killed my father at the ford last year. We do not know if they were Romans or Carthaginians. Both are equally bad."

"Get my hands free," Zonas begged, "if they pass, they may see us."

"It seems a pity to spoil the rope," Bassus said, fingering the knots, "it is better than what we have here."

"Cut it. It is one of my own."

"I do not think I can untie it." To his relief the boy knelt down beside him and began to slash the strands. "At least, not in time. I have been up in the hills with the goats and my grandfather should have brought food up to me yesterday but nobody came. Do you think the Numidians have killed him? There is no smoke and the yard is empty. I stood on a boulder and looked down but all I saw was Sikelia and then she suddenly disappeared."

"I thought I heard the howling of a dog."

"I knew Sikelia might have come back to the stable, that is why I came here to look."

"If there is no smoke, the soldiers may have left."

"Perhaps tonight I will crawl inside. I know a way to get in secretly through the barn."

"Water," Zonas pleaded and the boy gave him another drink. The trader's arms were now free but too numb for him to lift the bottle to his lips. "Is there a stream near?" he gasped.

"Yes, and I must go back to the herd. If the kids scatter I may not be able to collect them again before it grows dark. Besides, we are too close to the path here for safety. If I catch Sikelia you can ride her and I will give you some milk as soon as we reach my goats."

Zonas did not look back as the boy helped him onto the donkey, the mere thought of the hovel made him tremble. The beast was sure footed in spite of her size but he screamed once with cramp and Bassus snarled at him for making a noise, he had no strength left to beat the flies from his wrists and by the time that they reached the shelter of a rock beside a stream where the boy had left his cloak and an almost empty food bag, he was barely conscious and shivering with cold. He felt as if he were crawling up a hill, there was a shadow or was it a wolf, he could feel the fangs as it leapt at him and groaned. "Drink this," a voice ordered and a strange, bitter liquid burned his lacerated throat, his head cleared again and there was no wolf but only a dozen stars in the dark sky that reminded him of the grapes growing over the innkeeper's wall at Formiae. "It is what I give my goats," Bassus said, offering him the cup again, "there is nothing better for fevers."

Zonas woke unwillingly as Bassus tugged away the fleece that had been spread over his body. His wrists were sore but his mouth was less swollen and the crack on his head was beginning to heal. He drank some goat's milk, it was all that he was able to swallow and washed his face in the stream. "I found your hat," the boy said, holding it out, "it was lying on the grass near the hut but you can't have been wearing it, it isn't even torn."

"I took it off when the horsemen spoke to me," Zonas explained. He stroked the brim with relief, the rough, familiar grooves of the straw were as reassuring at that moment as meeting a friend in some unexpected spot. His first task was to get back to his servant and the sick mule. It was still early in the season and if he could hurry back to the port, friends would lend him enough to fill his bags again and this time he would keep to his well known, familiar roads. There was less to win on them but also less to lose. "Can you take me down to the village?" he asked.

"Come." Bassus took him by the arm and led him cautiously to the other side of the rock. The valley was full of Numidians, some were riding down the tracks and others had assembled in front of the huts. "I went up to the stable as soon as it was light," he said, "and that was when I found your hat but then I saw the soldiers and ran back here."

"They are using my bridles. The scoundrel who tricked me is leading them against his own people."

"Oh, the village is not worth looting. Besides, the Numidians have been in and out of it all winter. I think today they must be going to rejoin the main army. There have been only outposts here."

"Where is their commander?"

"The other side of the mountains. There is a path across, you must have seen it on your left as you came up."

"Are these all the animals you have?" Sikelia was hobbled near them, eating what happened to be a particularly tough thistle with enjoyment.

"Yes, we had an ox but my grandfather sold it last autumn to buy a little wine and pay our taxes. Taxes!" the boy laughed shrilly, "a fool in a white robe who had never picked a stone out of a furrow in his life took the remaining coins from my grandfather after the sale and told him he should be glad to pay for an army to protect him. Who has ever seen a Roman horseman when he was wanted? Besides, we have never been sure who the men were who killed my father."

Zonas nodded, it was a familiar story. The armies plundered, the farmers died, merchants starved, nobody sowed the fields. If Fortune had left him, what could he do himself? He had been seven years younger and the times had been quieter when he had first bought a mule and begun to travel alone. He shuddered, it was not only the poverty that he dreaded but the mingled scorn and commiseration of his comrades. Who could afford to be merciful while city after city was sacked and there was barley withering on the stalks because there were only ants left to harvest it? "What are we to do?" he asked, looking humbly at Bassus.

"The dog did not bark, I think they may have killed it. Yet the soldiers came sometimes in the winter and they paid for what they took. They may have warned my grandparents not to move until after they had left. I am going now to see what has happened to them. Wait for me here if you like."

Zonas hesitated. The fleece was soft, he was near water but the least sound made him jump and the long shadows of the grasses reminded him of ropes. Suppose Bassus did not return? "I will come with you," he said, suddenly afraid of being left alone, "but what are you going to do with the goats?"

"I shall leave them here. My grandfather forbade me to use this pasture before midsummer but today I cannot help it. Nobody can see it from the road, it should be safe."

They zigzagged up the slope that was shorter and less steep to the trader's surprise than it had seemed on the previous evening. There was nothing in sight but the smooth and sloping hills that even the donkey could not climb, except at one point where a landslide had cut a gash through the grass. The ascent in the sun started the trader's head aching again and he could not suppress a cry when they came in sight of the hovel. "Quiet!" Bassus said angrily, "the place may be full of soldiers."

The path turned towards a second valley where some smoke was rising from a few huts at the furthest, most visible point. "My kinsmen live there," Bassus said proudly, "my uncle is the smith. The Numidians must have protected you so as to get the bridles because the robbers in the village where you stayed would have cut your throat otherwise the first night."

"I had a token," Zonas touched it, the piece of leather was still hanging round his neck.

"This is our farm but I think my grandparents are hiding. If the Numidians were still there, we should see their horses tethered to the posts in the yard."

It was only a group of mud huts built inside a low wall. They would have called it a barn on the coast. Some hens pecked among the litter but otherwise there were no signs of life. "Nothing has been moved," Bassus said, pushing his hair out of his eyes, "there is still a pile of straw in front of the shed and a jug on the rim of the well."

"Perhaps your grandparents were afraid and went up to find you in the mountains?"

Bassus did not answer. He dropped to the ground and began to crawl quietly up the slope towards his home, looking exactly like one of his own, shaggy goats. Zonas stretched himself out beside a boulder. The climb had exhausted him, they had taken his knife, and his lack of speed would hamper the boy if there were any soldiers inside the house. He imagined, however, from what the grandson had said that the farmer had been selling his produce to the Carthaginians, and who was to blame him? They might spare the boy where they would kill the stranger. He tried to make himself as inconspicuous as possible but the grass was short, a slinger could see him easily from higher up the hill and he wished that he had stayed with the donkey, that Bassus would come back or that Fortune would send him a sign to assure him of her forgiveness.

If only he were sitting with his friends again! At this very moment the luckier fishermen would be sailing to the port with the morning wind. How he loved to watch them tumbling their catch onto the slabs at the corner of the fish market, with the colors not yet faded from the fins and the nets still sparkling with salt. If only he were back at Formiae, he would pick himself out something soft enough to swallow, a mullet perhaps and have it cooked with onion instead of pepper in the sauce and even a few mussels? The awnings would be up by now, the slave boys would be calling out the spices and he could sip a little broth while his fish was being cooked and . . . his eyes closed sleepily and he drowsed until he rolled over on his sore wrist and jumped. What miles of gaunt wilderness separated him from the coast.

He had learnt one lesson in this moment of pain, fear and starvation, only the present mattered. No memory of winter feasts would fill the hollow in his stomach nor an earlier security help him in his present danger. Where was Bassus? Had they seized the child? Ought he to crawl up, in his turn, and look for him? Everything seemed quiet, he had heard no sudden scream but obeying some blind impulse, he walked up to the wall and dropped, panting, beside it.

There was a sound of footsteps clattering without concealment across the yard. "They are dead," Bassus sobbed, "they are dead."

"The soldiers have killed them?"

"I don't know. I was afraid to look. They are covered with black spots."

"May Hermes protect us! Is it the plague?"

"My grandfather complained of a pain in his head. But that was when I left them five days ago." The boy was crying so noisily that something stirred in the corner and gave a feeble bark. It was the watch dog, tethered to a ring but evidently alive.

"And the Numidians?"

"There were none in the house."

"I had the sickness as a child," Zonas pointed to some scars on his face, "and they say the gods never strike a man with it twice." He had been one out of four survivors among the victims in his quarter and people had spoken of him afterwards as having "the luck of Hermes." Oh, why had he presumed on this so much? He stood here now, a beggar covered with cuts, because he had thought about sacks in his folly instead of buying the proper lamb.

"Loose the dog," the way that the animal tugged feebly

at its chain brought painful memories of his own struggle back to Zonas. "All it needs is water. And wait here till I come back."

The door stood open and, as the trader had supposed, all the objects were poor and rough. It seemed peaceful enough but Zonas hesitated at the threshold. What was that malignant smell in the air? In his still shaken state, he shivered, there was something evil abroad in the house.

The trader had often seen men killed during his years on the road but he started back in horror as he entered the room and the light from the doorway fell on the heap in the corner. An old man was lying with contracted limbs as if he had died in the utmost agony. Were the sores on the face a black eruption or merely flies? Zonas instinctively flung his arm across his mouth to mitigate the terrible stench. The woman had evidently perished first, her head had been covered by a cloak but one arm was stretched stiffly beside her and she was nearest to the hearth. The fire was out, a pitcher lay in fragments on the floor but there were no signs of any violence. A fly buzzed, Zonas thought that it was going to settle on him, he turned and fled, muttering a supplication for them all.

"Come," he shouted, "it's the black sickness, we are doomed if we stay here."

They raced towards the gate but just before they reached it Bassus stopped. "There's some meal in the barn," he panted, "I must fetch it, there is no food left."

The shed was empty except for some bowls in the corner, a pile of hay and a few baskets. Some odds and ends of harness hung on the wall. Zonas picked up a jar, it was lighter than he expected and he saw that it was only a quarter full of pulse. The boy thrust a pot into a hamper, snatched his spare cloak from a wooden peg and without waiting to shut the door they ran down the hillside, followed by the dog. "I never want to see our farm again," Bassus sobbed, "and yet we were happy."

They tore down the path without a thought of concealment. All that mattered was speed, to put as much distance between themselves and that smitten room as possible. Some figures were riding along the valley far below them but otherwise they were alone without a bird in the sky or a puff of wind in the grass. They came abreast of the hovel and Zonas slackened to a walk so that he could look at it again. Suffering made men childish, he reflected; he wanted now to fling open the door and stare inside at the spot where he had so nearly died although he knew it would not dislodge the memory from his mind but only increase its power.

"Numidians!" It was Bassus who perceived their danger, "run, I hear hooves behind us." He sprang down the slope and flung himself behind the nearest boulder. It was too low to give him much cover.

"The fattest lamb I can buy . . . the fattest lamb I can buy . . ." Zonas did not say the words aloud but they kept pace with his breath as he tried to flatten himself against the ground. Fortune had not forgiven him, he kept seeing the face of the old farmer rotting in that terrible room. What had life offered him and his wife? A few spring days when the sun melted the winter cold out of stiff bones, a harvest celebration at the nearest village once a year, a colored ribbon kept in an earthenware jar because it was too precious to be worn in the fields. They had got up with the light to water the cattle in summer, spent the dark January evenings lying on some old fleece without even a neighbor to cheer them with a tale and humbly brought the household gods (Zonas had seen the small, rough figures on a shelf) whatever they could spare: pulse, a saucer of milk, a garland of wild flowers. If a soldier had killed them wantonly but swiftly it would have saved them pain. At the very moment when he had been lying bound in the darkness, they had been screaming for the water that they were too weak to fetch. Oh, why had he also let the moments pass with the next year and another journey always in his mind? Lying here, waiting for the horses to thunder up to him, what did a full or empty belly, evil deeds or good, mean at the finish to a man about to die?

"They have dismounted, they are going into the court-yard," Bassus said eagerly, "we have just time to get to the shelter of the rocks."

A sudden wind rustled through the new grass. The tiny blue flowers growing between the stones like nails around a shield, were friendly and cool. How often the old farmer must have trodden this same path or looked up at that crooked peak facing them across the valley. Zonas felt too weak to run yet some instinct sent him struggling after the boy, his legs hurt, he could hardly drag one foot after the other, an open sore smarted on his lip. He stumbled, something whipped viciously round his ankle, he looked down, expecting to see a mountain viper whose bite here, without an antidote, would mean a slow and agonizing end. It was not a snake. A long strip of polished leather had hooked itself into the middle of a thistle. He bent down to pick it up and found another lying a couple of paces away. "A sign!" he yelled, "a sign!" They were some of his lost reins.

"Run!" Bassus beckoned to him wildly but Zonas did not crawl. He strode upright towards the boulders where the boy was sheltering. "I've found two of my bridles," he exclaimed, swinging them to and fro, "that scoundrel of a guide must have dropped them."

"Down!" The goatherd tugged at the trader's coat. "Do you want the Numidians to come and seize us?"

Zonas stretched himself obediently on the far side of a great stone. His despair had lifted, they were safe, Fortune's mercy was spreading as softly over his fears as his favorite Syrian balm would soothe his wounds if he had a pot of it with him. In June, on her feast day, he would sacrifice the best lamb that he could buy even if he had to live on pulse for six months afterwards.

"Ah," Bassus was on his knees, watching the farm through a cleft between the rocks, "they are running out as we did, they are afraid, they are racing each other for the horses."

Zonas nodded. He had so intense a conviction of forgiveness and that there was nothing more to fear except the ordinary hardships of the road that he hardly noticed what the boy was saying to him.

"The Numidians have stopped," Bassus continued in a puzzled voice, "they have not mounted. They are cutting down bushes."

Zonas rolled over and peered in his turn at the soldiers. One of them was huddled over a small depression in the ground, the other seemed to be walking towards the horses. "Perhaps they have found the traces of where I was robbed the other day?" he suggested.

"No," Bassus shook his head. "I saw the trampled grass when I fetched Sikelia's harness and picked up your hat. They knocked you down the other side of the path."

"Suppose they have found more bridles?"

"Then they would have picked them up and ridden away. Look! The other man is bringing some of our wood out of the yard. I think they are going to make a fire."

It was not a place where he would want to linger, the trader thought sleepily. Now that his fears had lifted, he longed to return to the stream. He felt feverish again, perhaps the boy would give him another draught of the medicine, bitter though it was, and later, a little milk. He dozed off finally, in spite of his aches, and woke unwillingly with the sun high overhead, as Bassus jerked at his coat. "Help me, Zonas, help me! They are burning the farm."

The two Numidians were standing outside the wall. Each carried a couple of flaming sticks. A spark must have fallen suddenly on one soldier's hand because he flung his torch with a yell of pain into the middle of the dry thatch. His companion hurried the length of the barn, setting the roof alight in a dozen places and throwing the brand finally into the middle of the flames. Then they turned, apparently in panic, and ran. This time they mounted the horses.

"Our farm!" Bassus sobbed, shaking his dark hair out of his eyes. He forgot caution and stepped into the open, shaking his fist and cursing all soldiers until Zonas grasped him firmly by the belt and tugged him into shelter.

"I must go," the boy struggled to free himself. "I saved you. Come and help me."

"Be quiet! Neither of us have weapons. You have still the goats and the land. Your kinsmen will help you rebuild the house once the armies have left and nobody could put the fire out now."

Bassus flung himself on the ground and buried his face in his hands until curiosity got the better of his grief and he stood up again, "my grandparents!" he moaned.

"They can feel nothing now. It is only a bigger pyre than we could have made."

"They cared for the flocks, they never missed an offering at a festival, it was small but it was all they had. Roman or Carthaginian, they plunder and burn and yet they are alive. Why are my grandparents dead?"

The trader felt too sore to try and reason out the motives behind man's destiny. Was it not enough that Fortune had relented and flung him back two bridles? "Come," he said, "the road is empty, let us go back to the goats before the blaze attracts another lot of horsemen to the neighborhood."

Bassus nodded, he wiped his face with the hem of his cloak and they started down the slippery grass slope by a zigzag path that Zonas had not noticed. They stopped sometimes to look at the farm. The flames were high, the litter was burning fiercely in the yard and there was a dull, reverberating sound as some stones fell forward into the well. "Why did they stop to burn it?" Bassus wailed.

It was merciful the trader thought, what man would have wanted to enter that terrible room? "An African sailor once saw these scars on my chin and told me that in his country they burnt the tents of any man who died from the black sickness as a sacrifice of appeasement."

"It was their cruelty." Bassus sliced off the top of a thistle with his knife. "I shall never forget this day and I will never forgive them."

CHAPTER 2

The place reeked of goat's dung and damp earth. Zonas yawned, he cursed his luck, the village and this inauspicious spring because no guide would take him to the next market town until the sowing was over. Till then, there was nothing to do but to idle away his time, spending resentfully the few funds that he still possessed and using his skill if they brought a galled beast back to the stable to earn himself an invitation to supper.

Even the weather had turned cold. The trader pulled a fleece that he had borrowed tightly about his shoulders. He had wanted to rejoin his servant but Bassus had refused to go to that particular valley, "it is the Numidian headquarters and they would cut our throats." It might be true but he suspected that after the destruction of the farm a feeling of homelessness had driven the boy towards his kinsmen. They had been kind but it was a poor, remote settlement and Bassus had accepted a farmer's offer to hire him and his goats the following day. He was terrified that his uncle might try to make a smith of him.

The stool Zonas was sitting on was hard and as he moved restlessly, a leg of it kept tilting on the uneven ground. The first great thankfulness of being alive and free was over, after his rescue he had thought that he could never be grateful enough for air and water but the mood had passed, he still repeated the words with his lips but the emotion had lessened. A hide flapped against a doorway and for an instant his longing for the coast was so great that he could have sworn he was listening to a sail being lowered or smelling a fresh fish soup instead of staring at a half starved donkey chewing the spines of a filthy clump of thistles. He had been crazy, it must have been that blow on the head but when Bassus had said he did not want the animal and a herdsman had given it a crack on the nose, he had remembered the inquisitive muzzle pushing open his prison door and had bought Sikelia although it had cost him the best of the bridles. She might become a useful beast with care and more food but the thinner and more decrepit she looked at the moment the safer it would be for both of them. He had stood over Bassus while the child exchanged the bridle for a thick cloak and a strong pair of sandals. "Save your wages and remain your own master," he had said to him at parting, "then with Fortune's help you will prosper."

It was a sullen landscape. Nobody had troubled to mend the great hole in the road, it was full of grit and decaying leaves. He wished that one of those forum philosophers who was fond of declaiming the virtues of the countryside could sit here instead of him, to choke in the dust and breathe the rancid stenches of the yard. Any rascal sleeping behind a barrel on the waterside was a richer man than these small farmers. They were avaricious and hard, one false step and they would stab him in his sleep as ruthlessly as any Numidian, nothing mattered to them but the increase in their flocks. There was no charity, no grace, not even the smith would send a cup of wine to a thirsty stranger as any of his friends would have done at Formiae. "Everybody would go on the road if they could," Zonas had repeated proudly since the spring when he had made his first journey and yet, he supposed, many could not bear the hardships and he knew that the real reason that Bassus had refused to join him as a mule boy was not the lack of wages but a determination to stay in the place of his birth.

Zonas yawned again, he touched the scar on his head with a cautious finger and stretched his legs out in front of him. "Pull, Buo, pull!" A shrill voice at his elbow made him turn suddenly. It was the headman's child, dragging some sticks to and fro and with a pebble tied in front of them for an ox, repeating in play what he was soon to do in earnest. "Is that the only game you know?" the trader asked but startled by his unfamiliar accent, the infant merely snatched his toy and ran away to another part of the street. The cold increased, it would soon be time to return to his evil, flea ridden pallet to toss there restlessly until it was light again. He had sworn up in the mountains that he would live every day in future to the full but existence in this grim and horrible place was a form of dying. He scratched his neck miserably, tried to kill a fly that had settled on his leg but missed it, almost upset his stool and leaned back uncomfortably once more against the wall.

A dog barked, the women stopped chattering at the fountain, somebody shouted. Zonas stood up and saw to his amazement a man, a slave and three mules, walking towards him up the path. He noticed with experienced eyes that the sacks were too full for there to have been many sales so that they could not have been long on the road but in spite of the dusty sandals and a mended leading rein, the sight was as impressive to him at that moment as a centurion leading a company of soldiers. Who was the fellow in front? Something about him seemed familiar. He was wearing a cloak of the specially fine wool that was usually reserved for stewards or landowners and Zonas had already seen it. "Dasius," he yelled, "Oh, Dasius! What are you doing in this forsaken valley?"

The man stopped. He seemed surprised (as well he might be) to hear his name.

"Don't you remember me? I am Zonas, son of Theodorus, and your master, Alfius, sold me a load of fodder last year."

Dasius stared, he was wondering who the dirty, battered figure in front of him could be? Then he recognized the trader's broad face under a battered hat. "What has happened?" He glanced round anxiously at the tumble down huts, "have you been robbed?"

"The Numidians left me for dead. I lost a mule but my donkey was grazing," Zonas lied, "I saved her and some goods."

"Numidians? Is it possible that there are any so far north? A landslide carried away the track and we have had to spend three days in a miserable village where nobody would speak to us, waiting for it to be cleared. Now we are on our way to Frusino."

"May I join you?" Zonas asked joyfully. His fears vanished, he forgot that he had ever called Alfius a fool for trusting mules to a man who so obviously disliked them; with luck, in a few weeks he would be in Formiae again among his friends.

Dasius hesitated. He had no intention of adding a man to the party who knew his master and could report the actual prices just as he was adding a coin or two here and there to his own bag. "We must march quickly to make up for the delay and you look too ill to risk the hardships of a journey."

Zonas stared, he expected mockery and he knew that in spite of misfortunes his comrades would drive a hard bargain for any help but there was a brotherhood of the road and it was the custom to help a man to reach the next town if he had been robbed. "My head has healed," he talked quickly as if he had not noticed the unwillingness, "but you had better remain here for the night. The next village is three hours away and it is already growing dark."

"Yes, master," the slave said eagerly, disregarding or not seeing a swift, cautionary shake of the head, "that was what the shepherd told us at the ford."

"Stay here," Zonas urged, "the people are rough but I have found them to be honest. We can leave as soon as it is light. I do not want to trade at Frusino but only to join a party there that is returning to the coast."

The prospect of having to spend an evening with the stained and tattered object in front of him repelled Dasius almost as much as the possibility that Zonas might spy on his sales. On the other hand, it was dusk and he had no wish to bump into a troop of Numidians. "Very well," he said without a trace of sympathy in his voice, "perhaps you can show us where we can stable the mules and then you can tell me your story while we eat."

"You left your servant alone in a strange village?" The pleasure of rebuking a man who was said to be one of the most experienced traders on the road almost made up, Dasius thought, for the undercooked and horrible stew that had been put in front of them.

"The headman's son pointed out the farm and it was near enough to get there and back in the day. I thought if I could sell a few of my goods, it would lighten the loads and we could get to Frusino more quickly. These villages are not exactly hospitable."

"My mouth is full of goat hairs," Dasius complained, "yet they charge me as much as if this were a kid. I wonder why Alfius sent me to this district? The people are as savage as wolves and the goods I have are no use to them." It was not strictly true because he had sold a bale of trinkets for double their value to his inexperienced customers; what they had refused to buy was the linen and the special oil from Histria.

"I am convinced that my mule was poisoned although I always turned over the fodder myself."

"They might have slipped some powder in the water. But why haven't you taken a guide here to get back to your servant?"

"Nobody will go. They say the place is full of Numidians. We saw at least thirty horsemen riding down the valley."

"Tell me again, you went with this party into the

hills?" Surely the trader could have got some woman in the village to mend that great rent across his tunic? He would have to get rid of him but he must listen patiently to the story or he might fall into an ambush himself.

"Yes, we traveled almost up to the farm," Zonas swallowed some goat hairs and spluttered.

"You were attacked where?"

"Within sight of our destination."

"If you were alone, I expect your guide signaled to the horsemen." Dasius leaned back against the wall and laughed.

"But I had an escort!" Zonas knew that it was unlikely that his companion could check his story. "I think they knew that there were soldiers in the mountains but had not heard that it was the day they were riding to rejoin their main camp. I was left for dead and only recovered consciousness when it was dark. By then, the farm was burning but a goat boy found me and brought me to his kinsmen here."

"It's the burning that I do not understand. The Carthaginian Commander is wise, he sees further than the Romans . . ." Dasius stopped abruptly, furious with himself for letting such words slip out.

"I know," Zonas agreed, "the Carthaginians pay for what they take. The Romans force the peasants into their army and there are not enough people left to gather in the harvest."

"So between the two armies nothing is left for us. Yours is a strange story, all the same."

"My head can prove that it is true. You can feel the hole if you like, I only took the bandage off yesterday." The trader leaned forward but all that Dasius could see in the smoky light from the brazier beside them was the zigzag line of a fresh scar.

"Oh, I am not questioning the fact that they knocked you down but why did they destroy the farm?"

It was the black sickness, Zonas was about to shriek, the house was cursed, but he checked himself just in time. He had warned Bassus to let his kinsfolk think that the horsemen had killed his grandparents lest at the mention of the black sickness they were thrown out of the village and stoned. "Somebody might have got drunk," he suggested, "or it could have been in a fight."

"What happened to you afterwards?"

"I crawled into a hut for shelter and a goatherd discovered me there the next day. He had been up in the mountains with his herd. We found my donkey but when I wanted to go back to my servant, the valley was full of soldiers so he brought me to his kinsmen here." He looked up at the blackened rafters of the low room and wondered if Dasius really meant to leave that strip of goat meat that he had pushed to one side of his saucer. It was tough but it was food.

"Fortune was with you," Dasius grunted. He was convinced as he looked at the eyes blinking in the smoke and the face that was green rather than white under the sunburn that the man was not telling him the truth. Had the fool gone there to make a bargain with the Numidians? He had let the remark pass about the Carthaginians having a better policy towards the farmers. "Oh well, as we say at Formiae, it's the small slip that brings the beating, not the forgotten deed."

"You will let me join you tomorrow until I can find a party going to the coast?" He would have to get up at dawn to stuff grass into the old sack that Bassus had given him so that he could pretend that Sikelia was still carrying some goods.

"And you crawled to a hut," Dasius said without answering the question.

"I crawled to a hut." Was it possible that a fellow trader was going to abandon him in this desolate village for all the people to know that he was friendless and poor? "As you remarked yourself, it is an inauspicious year."

"Yes . . . yes . . ." Dasius muttered impatiently, "but what sort of goods were you taking to that farmer? My packs are almost as full now as when we set out."

"Bridles." Zonas almost tipped backwards on his stool as he realized his mistake.

"Bridles! For a farmer!" Dasius smiled maliciously, he had now the proof he needed. "Special ones, no doubt, for special horses."

"They were ordered in Formiae," Zonas shrugged his shoulders, it might be better to be frank, "it was not my business to inquire why they were wanted."

"I am not blaming you. I should have done the same in your place but how could you have been so foolish as to take them up without a proper escort?"

"In such deals strangers are not welcome," Zonas said with a smile, he knew now that Dasius was curious if unfriendly, "besides I had the token." He had not thought of it for days but the emblem might still be useful.

"A token? Have you still got it with you?"

"Yes." The soldiers fortunately had not searched him. Zonas put his hand inside the neck of his tunic and after some fumbling pulled out the small, greasy slab of leather.

"It's a bit of their money," Dasius held it between the extreme tips of his fingers, "and worth very little."

"That was why it was chosen. A boy could have picked it up on any wharf, but turn it over. There's a special sign scratched on the other side."

"What will you take for it?" Dasius asked, handing it back and then wiping his hand carefully on an edge of his cloak.

"It is not for sale." The innkeeper's warning rang in his ears, "throw the thing away or you'll never come back to Formiae." Well, the lump had brought him no luck till this moment but now, with care, it might be a first step towards safety. "I wonder why you have never started trading for yourself," he said, looking at Dasius as if it were a matter that concerned him deeply. "Alfius knows costs and prices, I saw that when we were bargaining over the fodder last year but his summers are spent under a shady colonnade. What do you get out of all these dangers?"

"Nothing. He takes the profits and I live on greasy stews and sour wine." Dasius looked at Zonas with more compassion. After all, the man had merely been trying to get a coin or two to pay for all the extra tolls. Any trader might be robbed on these lawless roads and it might be his own turn tomorrow. Perhaps, after all, he would let the fellow come with him to Frusino.

"They say that only a couple of ships reached Kroton last summer and the Carthaginians are willing to pay double for all they need. Let me join you, we are Greeks, not Romans, and if Fortune favors us," Zonas poured the last dregs from his wine cup onto the floor and muttered a prayer, "we might put several pieces of silver into our bags. I made a mistake, I admit, in following the messenger instead of waiting for them to come to me but I did not trust the headman of that village."

"We shall have to find them again first."

"These people know more than they will admit but I think Frusino is better. We shall have to watch the men there buying oil. I have heard the Numidians will not fight without it."

"But you have no goods," Dasius objected.

"I have money deposited at Formiae." It was unnecessary to add that it was merely a couple of coins left with his friend, the innkeeper, so as to make sure of a lodging until he could walk round the market and dispose of his purchases at leisure. "Besides," Zonas leaned forward confidentially, "why tell Alfius the exact price if you sell the soldiers oil? We know what the villagers will pay and that is his due. If you risk danger yourself to get some extra silver, it is no concern of your master."

"Nor of the tax gatherer," and they both laughed.

"I have never had anything but tolls and curses from the Romans," Zonas grumbled, "I tramp the roads for six months of the year and they take half my earnings at the gates to fight a war where they usually lose the battles. And now I need another mule."

"They do not care what happens to us." Dasius leaned over and poured his own share of the wine into the trader's empty cup. The man was tattered and dirty but he was right. What had Alfius ever given him except a damp hole to sleep in during the winter and less wages than he had paid for one of the new fashionable Samian cups? Only if he got some silver between his fingers he would not spend it on a mule. Danger or not, he would use it to buy a passage to Iberia or Sicily, and set himself up in a town where nobody would refer to him as "that impudent bastard Sextus Cornelius brought back with him from Tarentum." He looked at the dirty straw where he would have to sleep that evening in disgust. "I am free born," he said unexpectedly and Zonas answered, "so am I." It had its advantages in the market.

"My mother was the daughter of one of the richest families in Tarentum. Her parents had more slaves than Alfius can count. Sextus Cornelius was a Roman and so the marriage was not recognized although our city was famous while they were mere herdsmen."

"But your father brought you up in his household and had you taught to read and write. You are fortunate. I have to rely on tallies."

"And died and left me so little that I had to hire myself out to Alfius."

"I wonder you did not find a place among the grain merchants."

"I thought of it but there was no chance there to be more than a clerk." He had had, perhaps, an exaggerated fear of the gossip that went around, "they call me ungrateful," he continued only half aware that Zonas was sleepy and not listening to him, "but if I made the least mistake in my studies, they called it Greek idleness and yet I learned twice as fast as the lawyer's two sons."

"I know," Zonas woke enough to nod solemnly, "but you can't go back to Tarentum. Hardly any ships call there now." The feel of a coin between his fingers meant more to the trader than the sting of any word.

"The Carthaginians are different. They admit no strangers inside their families but all merchants are equal in the market place."

"With this," Zonas held up the token, "we may make our fortunes."

"Yes." Perhaps it was the hours of walking and the airless room but everything began to sway until Dasius half felt and half imagined himself to be hanging on to a rope aboard a ship. A white city was rising from the water with white towers, white gulls, white sails. "Carthage, mistress of the seas"—that was where he wanted to be (he had only said Iberia for safety), there he would find neither mountains, nor hardships, nor Roman laws. He glanced round the smoky hut to where the headman in his work stained clothes, lay snoring beside the wall. "What would you do," he asked, yawning a little himself, "if you had, say, a piece of gold?"

"I should buy a piece of land and breed donkeys."

"First we must find the Carthaginians."

"And then get away before they cut our throats."

They laughed but both of them were dreaming by now and wanted to think about their own fables in silence. Zonas was too drowsy for once to verify Sikelia's halter. Tomorrow they would be on the road again, he dropped down on the straw and pulled the fleece across his legs, tomorrow there would be life . . . movement . . . hope. He wanted to lie there thinking about it all but his eyes closed and in another moment he was asleep.

CHAPTER 3

The grass was full of purple anemones, the scent of
everything green and growing was in the air, emerald
flashed as a lizard darted between two stones but Dasius strode forward at an increasing distance in front of
the mules without even noticing the plant of thyme that
he was crushing under his feet. His ears instead were
full of a voice that seemed faint, he supposed, because
it was so long since he had heard it. "Come out of the
sun, child, it brings fever." "Not to me, mother," he had
balanced himself proudly on the rim of a slab that
stood as if waiting for a statue to be placed on it. This
was how he would always remember her, alive, laughing, with a fleck of white, scarf or flower, in her dark
hair. "I know you're summer's boy, not mine, but I like

the shade, come and keep me company for a moment." Had he, he wondered, or had he tried to hit the fountain with his ball and then run after it?

"A captain told me that if I sailed south with him on his next voyage, we should come to a country where there is no grass and the ground is like the skin of an animal, powdered with gold."

"And you believed him?"

"Of course," he had never liked to be laughed at and he meant to travel one day and see the marvels with his own eyes, "but there are houses along the shore like our own."

He used these memories of his native city to protect himself from the miseries of the road. "Sleepy Tarentum" they had called it because the heat made people drowsy and nobody hurried along the wide streets unless a ship were moving in or out of the harbor. He had been older when they had sailed but he had felt no regret, his mind had been full of new sights and sounds and it had been a relief to get away from the women who had whispered whenever they thought him out of earshot, "she was afraid that Sextus would leave and take the boy, it was merciful she died." Destiny was destiny; "how old are you?" a sailor had asked when he had tried to catch the end of a rope and he had answered triumphantly, "I am nine." He stared round him now at the pasture where a cow was looking over its shoulder as if surprised that its own tail belonged to it; it and a damp warehouse were all that fate had tossed him for his pains.

"Da-si-us!" He looked round, if Zonas wanted to be taken as far as Frusino, the man would have to keep quiet. He wanted sometimes to take him by the throat and shake him till he could never hear those monotonous tones again, going on and on about loose straps, was a pinch of dittany good or bad for an ague, what they had eaten or were about to eat at each stopping place. The fool would die on the road, this year or next and he would have turned him loose already if it had not been for the token. He knew that Zonas had lied to him but part of the story was true, he had to put up with him, he had to pay for his food because that dirty bit of leather pressed into the right man's palm might mean that he could sell his oil at a high price to the Carthaginians. He stopped, pointed towards a clump of trees and motioned that he would wait there.

"Your master is impatient," Zonas said to the slave but the man had been well trained by Dasius. He shrugged his shoulders and was silent. The memory of the horsemen was too recent for the trader to be entirely at his ease but he had regained some strength and he was no longer, as they joked across the tables at Formiae, "afraid of shadows and unfit for the road." This was the moment of the day that he preferred, its small, incidental dangers were over, a village stood in front of them and every step was taking them closer to shelter and food. He trod on a branch of withered pine, it cracked and Sikelia turned her head. "I stopped to talk to an old woman," he said as they came abreast of Dasius, "because I wanted to know if that was truly a path there or just a ledge. It is a track and it leads across the mountains. Perhaps tonight we shall hear some news."

"News!" Dasius slapped a mule back into line as it tried to turn into a meadow, "all that they will tell us is that the lambs are few this season and that they are late in planting the beans."

Zonas nodded but he had caught sight of a black and orange web stretched across a twig and wandered over to see if it were a butterfly or a flower. Dasius flicked the mule with his switch although it was quietly moving along the path again, his companion's interest in trivial things irritated him beyond measure. What did it matter if there were three buds or five on the branches that they passed? It was the big stocks, the bales and barrels that mattered, things that could be sold for a real price, the handful of silver that would mean a place on a ship and a home in a new city that knew nothing of his boyhood.

A small wagon full of lumber came towards them from the direction of the village. Its driver was standing up in the cart, a stick in his hand. Two little girls drove a dozen particolored goats out of the way and then turned to look curiously at the strangers. "What do you want?" the man asked roughly as he came abreast of them, "we are poor here, we have no money for trinkets."

"We are on our way to Frusino," Dasius answered in a friendly manner, "is there an inn at your village where we can shelter for the night?"

"Frusino! You ought to be in the next valley. Take the second path to the left and you will come to a place where you can stop in about two hours." He looked round sullenly to see if his wheel would clear the bulging pack of the last mule.

"It is almost sunset and our beasts are tired."

"Our wine is finished, you had better do as I say." He flicked the oxen with his goad and went on without even a farewell salutation.

"How hospitable!" Dasius said and then added maliciously because the man had made him angry and he had seen through his companion's grass stuffed sack at once, "if his friends are like him, we shall get to Frusino when the market is over."

"Yes . . ." Zonas hesitated a moment as a confused recollection of a Numidian's smile and being dragged over rough, uneven ground flashed through his mind. His lips were dry, he could hardly frame the words but he managed to stammer, "did you notice the man's belt?"

"His belt?"

"There was an Iberian clasp on it. Of course," Zonas added hastily, "he could have found it in some market place."

"Here!" Dasius gave another angry blow to the flank of the nearer mule, he was furious that it had been Zonas and not himself who had noticed the buckle. "Of course, it is surprising how such trifles float about."

"They should not be short of wine. Look at the vines on that slope," Zonas pointed with a greasy finger towards the hill, "and now I can see a path as the old woman said, no, not there, about a hundred paces to the left."

"I shall say a mule is sick and stay here for a day."

"It is better to hurry to Frusino as soon as possible," Zonas said craftily, "otherwise, as you said, there will be no bargains left." He hoped that Dasius would delay because if they missed the market, it would give him an excuse to stay with him all summer and thus get back to Formiae without gains but also without debts.

Dasius stared at the vines. He longed to get rid of the trader who was dirtier and more unkempt than his slave. Yet it had been Zonas who had noticed the buckle and had realized that it was a sign that the man might have been bartering with soldiers in the hills. "One of my brooches is slightly damaged," he said, "a small stone is loose but nobody would notice it. I will give it to the headman for his wife and perhaps he will talk or you might hear something while you are tethering the animals." If he could not get away from the roughness and the stench he would soon lose his wits and the cry of the old doorkeeper at Tarentum came back to him, "yes, I have alms for you," he used to shout to the beggars, "but keep away from the steps. We don't want your fleas in the house."

The inn was better than the others where they had stayed and, in spite of the warning, the wine was plentiful and good. Dasius was in such an unexpected good humor that he had ordered a chicken. "There have been strangers here," he said when Zonas joined him, "but they seem to have been traders like ourselves, buying fodder for the Roman army."

"They know something but they will not talk," Zonas said lazily, reaching for a second piece of fowl. He was wondering whether the reason why his wound took so long to heal was not simply hunger? He yawned and was glad that Dasius had not noticed this, having turned his head at that moment to ask a woodcutter where the path led over the hills? It was too abrupt and naturally the man gave him an evasive answer.

"You say you do not care but I believe you think the Latins will win in the end," Dasius grumbled, putting down a bone and wiping his plate with a bit of bread.

"Carthage speaks with many voices, Rome with one. A captain told me last winter that the Punic merchants voted against sending more elephants here."

"Their Commander has looted no cities recently and

tnerefore has not filled the Treasury with gold. I don't remember the captain. Where did you meet him?"

"Why, in Formiae. You were sitting at the next table yourself. Don't you remember? He was always smiling and that particular day, he had a little monkey on his shoulder."

"Of course, of course," Dasius gulped some wine so hurriedly that he almost choked, why must it be his ignorant companion who saw and recalled so exactly the incidents of each day? "The innkeeper tried to buy the beast and he said he would not sell it for a denarius. I thought he came from Rhegion."

"He had not come from Carthage itself, there are too many Roman galleys watching the seas but he knew that coast."

"Oh, it's always 'he had known' or 'he said he had spoken to an African' but we never meet anyone who has actually seen a Carthaginian," Dasius said too loudly, banging the table in exasperation, "I begin to think they do not exist."

"Listen!" Zonas sprang to his feet, he had heard the scrape of many sandals on the cobbles. He turned just as the room filled up with soldiers. "Be still," a stern voice shouted in Latin, "stay where you are and no harm will come to you." A man stepped forward with a torch and its light fell across the emblem on the officer's leather jacket. These were no raiders. They were Carthaginian infantry from the main body of the army.

"We are camping tonight in the fields around your village," the officer continued in an easy, almost accent free, voice. "Go at once to your homes and nobody will interfere with you if you stay indoors till it is light. To-morrow is a feast day for us and you may watch our troops march past after the sacrifice. If you have wine or meat to sell, you can meet me here afterwards. But I warn you," he shouted now as if he were giving an order to his soldiers, "if you try to slip away to the hills, our slingers are posted round the fields and they are merciless. Stay where you are and you have nothing to fear. We shall pay for what we need."

The soldier with the torch took up his position at the door. A peasant forgot to finish his half filled cup, another stood as if paralyzed with his hands clasped behind his back. "To your homes," the officer repeated in a loud, sharp voice, staring at Dasius who was better dressed than any of the villagers. Zonas finished his wine and snatched up a loaf of uneaten bread. "Come," he said, noticing that Dasius was turning towards the Carthaginian, "leave your bargaining till the morning. They are watching us and wondering who we are."

CHAPTER 4

Dasius yawned. They would have to wait at least another hour but since sunrise every man, woman and child who could walk had begun fighting for places along one side of an almost level field outside the village. A few soldiers were keeping them reasonably in line and ordering the watch dogs to be securely tied up in the yards. The army itself was some distance away but they could hear the thud of the poles as the tents were struck and presently a priest's voice rose in the clear air. "You are lucky," a guard said who spoke a little of their language, "there will be a parade after the sacrifice and then the army will march to the river."

Zonas fidgeted from one foot to the other. They had not let him tie Sikelia up himself and he knew what slaves could be like. There was a certain knot that she was crafty enough to undo and if she wandered away he might not find her before nightfall; Dasius might leave, a wolf might get her. Besides, he was still weak and did not want to go stumbling about slippery hillsides in the dark. He had also known stablemen deliberately let beasts stray in order to demand a reward for catching them and bringing them back.

"Don't look so gloomy," Dasius said, "I have never seen the Carthaginians parade and they say it is a magnificent spectacle, as fine as the opening of the Corinthian Games."

"It's Sikelia. Suppose that fellow has tied her up carelessly? I've known her wriggle out of her halter before."

"Other people can look after animals besides yourself," Dasius teased. It was true that the trader knew more about mules than about bargains but this preoccupation with his wretched donkey was a nuisance.

"Keep back!" A guard pushed one small boy against his father's knees and cuffed a second too eager one on the ear.

A trumpet sounded. It echoed among the peaks around them, the people stood still. "The sacrifices are over," the guard explained, "keep in line and if you are lucky you will see the elephant with his tower."

"The elephant!" One of the children began to wail.

"You are safe here." The guard turned and faced them good humoredly, "keep still and the beast will not harm you. You may cheer if you like when the Commander passes," he added graciously, "you will know when he arrives because his personal bodyguard will be riding in front."

Zonas was still uneasy. He looked up and down the

rows of brown, weatherbeaten faces and wished he was sure of Sikelia being in her stable. The women had put on their festival clothes, here and there he caught sight of a scrap of yellow ribbon or a white robe fastened with one of the cheap brooches that Dasius sold to the peasants. "A gift for your wife," he would suggest after the main bargaining was over, "a head of Juno to bring your household luck or a winged Minerva straight from Greece?" They were all made, of course, from rough molds at a pottery near Neapolis.

"The Carthaginians understand people," Dasius murmured in a low voice. "These people will talk about the spectacle all winter. The Romans would say they ought to be at work. Hannibal knows that they will never forget him."

"The Greeks would have done this too," Zonas protested.

"But they would have charged everybody for a place."

"And we might have gained a few drachmas. All the same, Dasius, I feel we shall have to pay for this in some way, I wish it were over."

There was little talk unless a man thought that his neighbor was pushing him out of his place. A baby began to cry and some other infants started to quarrel. "Keep those children quiet or take them away," the guard ordered and there was instant silence.

The trumpets sounded a second time. Zonas glanced up at the pastures. They were smooth and soft and reminded him of an Ionian who had made a pavement for the judge's villa at Formiae from oblongs of stone that were just the same green. The craftsman had needed the patience of the gods to finish his work but it had looked as real as a garden afterwards and, as he had said, did not turn brown in summer. There was no movement above them of man or beast. Surely some shepherds had stayed with their flocks? "Up there," Dasius nudged him and he discovered two dots on the right of a crag; they had crooks in their hands and were staring down at the valley. Only the sheep had their backs turned to the village.

There was a sound like a stream falling over a cliff, there was a cloud of light dust. "They are coming!" The word passed instantaneously along the crowd, fathers swung their children onto their shoulders, girls linked arms so as not to be pressed out of line. "When I salute the second time, cheer," the guard commanded, stepping a pace forward.

"They are coming!" This time it was a joyful shout. A row of Numidians with exactly the same distance between each horse (it was so precise that Zonas could have used it as a measuring rod for his cloth), trotted into view. The round shield that every soldier carried on his left arm, the faces under the leather caps, were as dark as the animals that they rode and as the sunlight caught the massed points of the moving darts, these danced and shimmered as if they were under water. "The ponies are from the Apennines," Dasius whispered, "or perhaps from Gaul, their desert horses, I suppose, are dead."

The small boys squealed with joy as the first rank drew abreast of them but as he caught sight of the javelin in the nearest rider's hand, Zonas felt the scar twitch on his scalp and took an involuntary step backwards. "My foot, you fool, my foot!" a woman yelled and he felt a sandal kick him hard at the back of the leg. "They say that the best horsemen come from the West," Dasius continued, unaware of his companion's clumsiness and

Zonas answered eagerly so as to escape looking round at the angry female behind him, "yes, but they admit no strangers and if any try to go there, they lose their way and die in the sand."

There was a pause while the dust settled and people began to talk again in low, excited tones. "It is not horse and rider but a single being," the innkeeper's wife declared, "just like the statues at Tibur."

"Don't drag Tibur into everything, mother," a voice yelled from the back of the crowd. "We know you have been there without your telling us about it every day, besides you can't compare Numidians with the figures on the colonnade."

"And the Romans ask us to stand up against might like this!" a farmer wailed.

"I would!" a boy shouted from somewhere in the group and the guard turned sharply to see who the speaker was. "Be quiet, you would be the first to run," an old man said hurriedly, "remember my sheep dog, you thought it was a wolf." There was a yell of laughter although the boy clenched his fists. "You are right," Zonas whispered, "the Carthaginians are as cunning as us Greeks. Rome will get no levies from the villages here."

"The Iberians!" A farmer stepped abreast of the guard in his excitement and was angrily pushed back. The slingers were wiry fellows with immense shoulders because they had to combine great speed with the ability to carry a bag of heavy stones. According to rumor, they were the toughest unit in the army, recruited from such arid plains that they were able to go for days without food. "Is it true that they can live from the dew on their pebbles and that if they are starving, they make a paste out of dust?" Dasius said, half mockingly, to the guard.

"We leave them alone," the soldier answered tolerantly, "they seem to prefer to sit with each other in the wine shops but I have never known them backward in snatching either loot or food."

"Oh!" The crowd roared in admiration as the backbone of the army appeared, veterans from the earlier Iberian campaigns, men from Carthage itself. Their swords were belted high so as not to interfere with the marching step, their shields were strapped to their backs, their casques fitted closely to their heads. Some were survivors from the passage across the Alps, most of them were dark with here and there a fair haired Gaul. "The sands are a good nursery for endurance," Zonas muttered but his companion did not reply. Dasius was staring at a sword, it was Roman from its weight and he noticed that the man's shield had been slashed in two and clumsily mended. Slowly, rank by rank, the Carthaginians passed the dusty, waving onlookers with the arrogance of men so conscious of their worth that any part of the world would seem their kingdom.

"A party will stay behind tonight to clear up after the sacrifice," the guard said, pushing a child forward so that it had a better view. "They will tell you stories such as you will never hear again in your lives if you give them a jug of wine."

"Oh, look! The officer has a wolf's head on his shield," a small boy yelled and his mother hushed him anxiously.

"Yes," Dasius whispered, "they march as if this were a triumph and not an ordinary parade. What can the Romans do against them when most of their levies cannot even keep in rank?"

Zonas shrugged his shoulders. If the Carthaginians had won the battles, they had not conquered the land.

"Neither city wants us as citizens," he grumbled, "and yet we have as much right to air, a portion of meat and a coin or two for our old age as any of these strangers." His head buzzed, a fly settled on his neck that he could not slap away because they were so closely pressed together and as he thought of the spear butt and his lost bridles, his anger rose and he hated them, soldier, peasant, Dasius, the guard, with the same sullen dislike.

"Back!" Two men had surged across the line to admire the swords. "You are about to see what few people can watch unless they are about to be killed. Here comes the elephant."

It advanced alone, its forehead protected by a piece of armor as wide as a man's shield, the enormous ears flapping as it walked. "Why, its feet are the color of thunder," Zonas muttered, thinking of the dark skies of a sudden summer storm. The black face of the African driver grinned at the crowd. There were four archers behind him in the high basket-like turret but his solitary weapon was a light, polished stick. "How well it is arranged," Dasius whispered, "the peasants are trembling, I am almost frightened myself, then after the beast has passed, the Commander will ride by, the elephant's master, the only one that can order it to charge."

The driver touched the animal's neck. It turned slightly to the left and nearer the villagers. "Keep quiet and it will do you no harm," the guard shouted facing his charges. One or two children who had covered their faces with their hands, ventured to peep through their fingers. A word. The trunk lifted slowly into the air. It hovered, it took a straw hat from an old peasant as the people screamed and then, at a second command, laid it beside him on the ground again. "It is teaching you your manners," the guard said gaily, "how can the women behind you see the procession?"

The elephant moved away into the center of the field. "It has a gold badge," the innkeeper's wife said in surprise. "But it's not as swift as a horse," the peasant objected, brushing the dust off his hat. "You should see them in battle, they . . ." the guard stopped and there was a yell from the crowd. Something, it was not much bigger than a dog, was charging towards the elephant. "Sikelia!" Zonas yelled, "Sikelia!" The idiot had tied the wrong knot as he had feared and her halter was trailing behind her on the ground.

Zonas could never remember afterwards what actually happened. A force of some kind exploded in his head. It was his donkey, the beast that had saved him from dying of thirst and pain, the only means by which he could return as a free man to his town. He did not hear the roars, he saw only Sikelia and knew that they were about to kill her. He smashed the guard's arm aside, he raced towards the startled elephant waving his mule stick at its bulk and tried unsuccessfully to grip the halter wriggling along the grass as if the donkey were a puppy and the beast an old wagon horse turned out to pasture.

Behind and about him the line yelled with laughter. "He's a tumbler," somebody shouted, "a tumbler from Kroton."

"A coin for my master!" One of the soldiers imitated the whine of a juggler's slave boy.

"The elephant has mated with a dolphin and here is its calf!"

"No, the gods have stricken the man, he has lost his wits."

Nobody noticed the cavalry ride up until an Iberian

stepped forward, a sling in his hand. He looked up, waiting for an order. The African, cursing, succeeded in stopping his beast in the middle of the field. The donkey was still trotting towards the swinging trunk but Zonas reached her at that moment, trod on the halter, snatched it up and pulled her back. A stern command rang through the slackening laughter. "Bring them both here."

Two soldiers twisted the trader's arms behind him and led him forwards at a run. A third took the donkey's rein. Dazed and as if waking a second time from fever, Zonas saw a horse in front of him, a Libyan, judging from the high neck and its dark color and he did not need to glance at the short, red cloak nor at the gilded lion that seemed about to jump from the center of the shield, to know that he was in the presence of the Commander himself.

"So," the rider said, "you are not afraid of my elephant?"

At a sign, the soldiers released Zonas who dropped to his knees in supplication. "But I am terrified of it," he said, and now it was true.

"Yet you followed your donkey with only a stick."

"She is all I have." He dared not look up, his eyes were fixed on the horse's hooves and the only thought that flashed across his mind was surprise that he had dared to buy those ten bridles. Must a man's faults always pursue him till he died?

"Let the man have his beast. He has given us a good laugh."

Zonas lifted his head, too stunned to utter a word of gratitude or thanks. If that voice had ordered him to take a sword and follow him to the mountains, he would have marched till he dropped. It was not the force behind him nor his army. He had understood the struggles of a ragged, despairing peddler, and such a man, if given a chance, could change the world.

He heard an order, an attendant dropped something into the trader's hand, the horses raced by him in a cloud of dust and Zonas stared at the coin in his palm as if it too might vanish. It was silver and bore the impression of the Commander's head.

"You owe Fortune something," a man grunted, thrusting Sikelia's halter into his hand. "I crossed the Alps and fought at Trebia for less." Then as his wits returned Zonas began to tremble all over. He had struck a guard, he had charged an elephant and instead of putting an arrow through him, they had given him the price of an ox. "Yes," he said, looking earnestly at the soldier, "I swear, I swear at the next Lupercalia I will offer the fattest sheep I can buy."

CHAPTER 5

If he closed his eyes, all Zonas saw was a wrinkled foot
the size of a battering ram ready to crush him. He was
exhausted by his adventure yet he dared not take his
ease in the smoky room that was full of soldiers and
admiring villagers. The episode had amused the men
and they kept on asking him to drink with them. Usually he would have been glad enough to join them but
suppose tonight he provoked them by some chance or
careless word? They might clout him on the head again
and he would find in the morning that both the stater
and his donkey had disappeared.

"Salute, Elephant Tamer!" An Iberian opposite
laughed and raised his cup.

"Oh, he was born in Carthage or he would have been

afraid of the beast." Several of the soldiers had decided, in spite of his denials, that he was a Greek merchant come from Africa and it was useless to tell them that a sudden, blind rage had wiped all sense of danger out of his mind.

"I am so small," he joked back, "that I thought it would take me for a fat mosquito."

The group burst into another roar of laughter and one of them slapped him so heartily on the shoulder that his head started aching again. All that he wanted to do was to lie down and sleep.

"There's my evening wine gone!" The luck of the game had shifted against him and a man flung the knucklebones angrily to the floor. "When are we going to give up this moving and marching? It's years since we had even a small town to loot."

"It may be good for our legs but it's cold." A dark skinned African pulled his cloak round his shoulders and rubbed his hands.

"I could do with a coin or two myself," a man next to Zonas wiped some wine drops off his belt with a bit of rag, "but then I should stay here. There is water and grass."

"You are not a Numidian?"

"No, I come from the plains beyond the Ebro and water was as rare in our village as the silver I should like to stuff inside my fist. I suppose you won't believe me but I never saw real streams till I got to Gaul. If I could buy a piece of land with a river full of rushes running through it, I would give up soldiering and settle here."

"Oh, not rushes. They make too good an ambush for the enemy. The first thing I should do would be to cut them down."

"They are useful to us as well." The speaker was another Iberian because there was a broad band of unfaded cloth across his tunic where the slinger's bag of stones had been suspended from his shoulder.

"I am always uneasy when I am near reeds."

"They helped us at the crossing of the Anio," the Iberian answered impatiently, "we hid among them to keep the Romans from your flank while you crossed the river."

"The Anio! I shall not forget that day in a hurry," a Numidian drained his cup and put it on the table in front of him. "I got a javelin through my arm in the middle of the crossing but fortunately it did not cripple me. I was thinking of all the loot we had missed in Rome when it struck me."

"I shall never understand why we marched away from the city."

"It was full of soldiers, you fool, besides, our masters in Carthage were anxious about their corn fields in Sicily."

"They promise us horsemen and more elephants but the troops never arrive." The fair haired Gaul spoke with an accent and Zonas noticed that the man's fingers were always playing with something, his wine cup or the silver badge on the great leather coat that lay across his knees.

"We were victorious. We were about to have a triumph and suddenly we were splashing across a river with the Romans on top of us. All I know is that I am thankful we had no elephants with us then or we should have been killed while they were trying to get the beasts across the ford. They won't move unless they can feel their foothold."

"You forget!" The Iberian pointed to Zonas who had

wriggled as far away from the soldiers as he dared into a dark corner filled with cobwebs. "We should only have had to send for our tamer and he would have led the elephants across after his donkey."

"If you knew how frightened I am of them!" Zonas pretended to tremble and they laughed until the Iberian leaned over and filled up the trader's cup again.

"Elephants are splendid in their· proper place," the African said angrily as if he had been personally insulted. "They need sand. They are useless here, the food isn't right and they cut their feet on the rocks."

"All that I remember of the Anio is wading through the water among carcasses of horses and a few of my own friends. Where you slingers were, I'll never know. The first I saw of you was when we camped and that was two days afterwards."

"We were on your flank, keeping the Latins away. I lost seventeen of my comrades in an hour."

"The Romans fight well but they are stupid."

"Orders or no orders, I still wonder why the Commander kept us from looting Rome."

"The levies were out, our losses would have been tremendous."

"And our plunder the greater, it would have been the end of the war."

"Soldiers are cheap," the African bellowed, tilting himself backwards and forwards on his stool.

"It is more than six months since we were paid. My cloak is in rags and it is chilly in these hills."

Zonas, who had been drowsing, woke up like a good trader in time to hear these words. Soldiers often pretended that they had not received their pay in order to make a better bargain but it was unlikely that these men were lying, sitting at ease among themselves. They yawned, they had spent their few coins and drunk all the wine that the villagers had offered them; one by one, they started to leave for their camp. A figure beckoned to Zonas from the door. He slid out of his corner and joined Dasius in the courtyard. "The peasants have been telling the truth," the trader said, pulling his cloak round him because it was really cold, "the soldiers have not been paid since last autumn."

"Their Commander is a wise man. He gives them their wages only after the campaigning season is finished. They spend them while in winter quarters and are ready to fight again in the spring. I admire him, he is not obstinate like the Romans, he varies his plans to meet the times."

"Yes," Zonas felt instinctively for the stater underneath his coat, "all the same I shall be thankful to see Formiae again. We can leave for Frusino tomorrow, I suppose, or have you still business here?"

"I have not wasted the evening," Dasius was glad that Zonas could not see his face in the darkness because he could hardly conceal the contempt he felt for his companion. They could both have been flogged or even killed that morning if the soldiers had not laughed. He must get rid of the fellow at the earliest opportunity. "I spoke to the officer and he bought my oil. I like the Carthaginians, he never once yelled 'slippery as a Greek' at me and he paid a reasonable price. The jars have to be weighed tomorrow but we can leave for Frusino immediately afterwards."

"I am glad," Zonas said with relief, "I shall be afraid of Numidians till I die." All the same, what stories he would have to tell his friends and he could see the innkeeper's face turning into a solid wrinkle of amazement when he said, "and, you know, the beast's foot was the size of the pediment in the forum." Only, he tried to check his thoughts, he must not dream about how he would astonish them until he was safely inside his own town or he might anger Fortune again, there was the sheep to buy first and a long, dangerous journey that would start in the morning. He yawned again and followed Dasius gratefully towards their sleeping place at the back of the tavern.

CHAPTER 6

Zonas sat in front of the hut, making a new hole in Sikelia's girth. The donkey was filling out nicely now that she had better food. It was late, he had overslept but Dasius had wakened him to tell him that the army was on the move and so he need not hurry, "the villagers sold so much meat last night that some of them are going to Frusino to spend their gains. I have arranged for us to join them but they are not leaving till noon. Wait here. My slave and I will fetch the animals, they are grazing beside the stream."

His hand went towards his chest but Zonas drew it back with a jerk. It was both childish and dangerous to keep feeling for the coin. Once he got to the coast there was a rough bit of land that he might be able to buy, there was water running through it and good pasture for the mules. It would take him a few months to grub out the willows and mend an old shepherd's hut on a bit of higher ground but it had two other advantages; it was close enough to Formiae to be safe and it was off the main road. He might even have enough left to buy himself a slave, some woman who would cook for him and bear him sons. To know the right fodder for the different beasts a boy should begin his training as soon as he could walk. The sun was on his back and he was beginning to feel drowsy again when a boy came running towards him. The figure reminded him of Bassus, the same dark, almost goat like hair fell over a brown forehead. "Dasius, the trader, asked me to give you this," the messenger said, thrusting a small piece of cloth into his hands. "I am to tell you that he left with the Carthaginians but he advises you to go with our party to Frusino, the mountain journey would have been too severe with the wound on your head still unhealed. He prays that Fortune may protect you and that you will return safely to your home."

Zonas tore open the cloth in a rage, it contained the now useless leather token. "Our men are almost ready to leave," the boy added with a malicious grin, "shall I fetch you your donkey?" Zonas nodded, unable to speak. The traitor! He knew that Dasius despised him for his rough jokes and the way he ate but he had cured the pack sore on the best mule's back and who had seen the buckle first on the wagoner's belt? There was nothing that he could do, by now Dasius had had at least an hour's start but let them once meet again in a market place and he would tell the rogue in front of the crowd exactly what he thought of him. He thrust a coin in the urchin's hand when he came back with Sikelia and told him to fetch the sacks. The grass had gone, he had thrown it out on the previous day. Some of the soldiers had flung him small coins as a joke. Dasius would have left them on the ground but he had suffered too much to be proud, he had picked them up and exchanged them in the village for bread and a couple of slices of dried meat.

Three men came down the road, leading their animals. They nodded sullenly, he gripped Sikelia's halter and followed them out of the village. There were bare patches on the fields where the army had camped. They chose the first of two well worn tracks that led towards the valley but Zonas stopped at the corner and looked at the opposite hills. The last men of the Carthaginian rearguard were riding up the pass. Their helmet plumes rose and dipped, dipped and rose, like a flock of colored birds. Dasius was already out of sight. Zonas shook his fist at the cloud of dust yet he smiled to himself in spite of his anger. A trader would be kicked from tent to tent by the soldiers whereas he would soon hear the innkeeper's voice bellowing a welcome and feel the familiar Formiae cobblestones underneath his feet.

It was, Zonas supposed, the luck of the road. He had often joined other traders for part of his journeys and he missed their warm comradeship. They would have done their best to outwit him in a bargain but they would never have abandoned him in an almost hostile village. He had seen at once that the peasants had no intention of taking him to Frusino. They had suspected that he might betray them to the Romans. The fools! How could he explain his possession of the stater to some suspicious official? These silver coins with their portraits of the Carthaginian commanders came straight from the Iberian mines. They had stopped for the night at a small farm and he had refused to leave the stable. He had not dared to sleep but had slipped away at the first signs of dawn in an opposite direction. He would lose a day through not being able to take the direct road to the market but he had noticed a valley on the previous evening that should lead through a low range of hills to the town.

Zonas stopped every few paces to glance over his shoulder and started if he kicked a pebble. The ground was already parched, there were few plants and a gritty dust burned through the soles of his sandals. His friend, the innkeeper, was right; a trader was as much a beast of burden as his mule, scenes and scoldings tumbled through his mind as he dragged himself across the stones that were plentiful enough to please a company of slingers. Why had they beaten him so hard on his first journey because he had not found that piece of bramble at the bottom of the hay? It had been full of thorns but nobody had told him to sift the fodder before turning it into the manger. Ought he to have listened to the sailor who had bought a pot of honey from him, "come with us, the sea is better than a dusty path." Yet there was also the exhilaration of each new expedition, the knowledge that he was his own master, the mornings in the early spring when even the dust seemed scented. If it were not for the soldiers, Roman as well as Carthaginian, if a man could ride from south to north with nothing to fear except the discomforts of the inns, who would ask more than a few good bargains and a chance to follow the mules?

It was hot, Zonas felt a headache coming on and naturally, because of this, his thoughts went back to that terrible hut. The scars had not quite faded from his wrists and as he looked about him for a stream, his companion's mocking "but your wound is still unhealed" echoed in his ears. "That scoundrel!" he said aloud, whisking some flies from Sikelia's ears and yet, for all his anger, he missed Dasius more than he would admit. The fellow had known so much, his stories had eased the marches during the dreary afternoons, besides, he had given him an excellent remedy against fleas. It was early in the day but almost against his will, he flopped down sleepily beside what had seemed to be a bush but was actually an unusually large stem of asphodel and stretched his legs in front of him. Not even a stater would last a lifetime and what would happen if he lost his strength and could not even make the round of the placid villages along the coast? Try as he would, the thought of a graybeard to whom he had once given a meal haunted his mind. "My belly is still my master," was all that the man had said by way of thanks, "but I should have had the courage to refuse your alms. I shall be better off in the shades." It had taken three bowls of wine even then to wipe away the memory of that gaunt and suffering face.

He heard a rustle, something touched his hand. It was merely a lizard but Zonas jumped to his feet and snatched Sikelia away from a particularly juicy thistle. Had he forgotten his cunning? This spot was open, he could be seen from either side of the valley. He climbed to the top of a boulder and looked about him. There was a stream but the mountain snows had not yet fully melted and there was only a trickle of water near at hand. It would be deeper by the bed of rushes that he could see some distance away and above it there was a row of bee hives, no, they must be huts, clinging to the side of the hill in a shallow cleft. One or two men were working on the slopes and he wondered if he dared ask one of them for shelter? He had kept his rags although Dasius had bought him a half worn out coat and with his dirty sacks he looked what he actually was, a peddler of the poorer kind driven from his usual markets by the army. "The horsemen scattered us. I was a little behind my companions at the time, hitching up my donkey's girth and so I hid in a ditch. Afterwards, I did not know where they were and lost my way." It was almost true and if he held up a copper coin and said that he had friends at Frusino, they would probably let him sleep in a barn and set him on the right path in the morning.

There seemed to have been a landslide at some earlier time because hummocks of stone stuck out of the grass and the track ended abruptly. Zonas picked his way cautiously from rock to rock and promised himself a rest when he got to the water. He had almost reached the grass on the further side when he trod on something hard that did not give under his foot. He glanced down, it was the hilt of a small, broken dagger and as he stooped to pick it up, he saw the hand that had held it, protruding between two boulders.

The trader jerked Sikelia's halter in terror. He looked right and left and then, hearing no sound, dropped to his hands and knees and began to crawl as gently as possible round the rocks. A youth was lying in a hollow between them, apparently asleep, with his head towards the river. He was wearing a Roman corselet but there was no sign of either helmet or sword. There were plenty of hoof prints on the damp ground but no marks of struggle where the youth was lying although even the quiet movement that Zonas made lifting himself over a small, flat slab that barred his way, disturbed a cloud of flies. Then he saw that the boy's shoulder had been smashed by a stone, thrown, no doubt, by an Iberian.

Zonas looked round again. The men were working quietly in the fields on the slope above him and it seemed likely that the blow had been the result of some chance shot rather than a deliberate raid. Perhaps the Carthaginians had sent a couple of slingers to explore the valley? If so, they would have left immediately after seeing the Roman fall. He knelt down and began to cut away the coat. It was kinder to do this while the youth was unconscious.

Zonas was not an imaginative man, he was not irreverent but he had always said that if he joined a temple procession it was for the sake of the meat and drink distributed afterwards to the worshipers, yet as he cleaned the fragments of stone and leather from the wound, it seemed to him that he was bending over the figure of some favorite of the gods such as he had seen in the pictures in the atrium at Formiae when he had delivered some oil to the judge's villa. "May Apollo help me," he muttered, running his hand over the uninjured lower arm. Here was the difference between his animals and mankind. Sikelia followed her instincts but muscles such as these were conscious of how they were used.

The figure writhed as he cut away the last remnant of the leather strap. "Softly," Zonas muttered, treating the fellow exactly like a mule in spite of the thoughts that had been running through his head, "don't move. I will bring you a bowl of water presently and dress the wound with balm." He was glad that he had bought some in one of the villages before Dasius had left him.

"Orbius!" the boy muttered, "Orbius!" He struggled back to consciousness and tried to sit up.

"Quiet!" Zonas forced him gently to the ground again. "Was it a solitary slinger or a band of raiders?"

"Orbius!" It was a groan rather than a word. "They must have killed him."

"How? Where?" Zonas glanced uneasily around again. All was summer, all was quiet.

"We were sent with ten horsemen to search the valley. The peasants denied having seen any Carthaginians, they always do. The enemy pays more for the corn and they forget that we are fighting for them. It seemed so peaceful that while the men were collecting the horses, Orbius and I went to bathe. I suppose we must have wandered out of sight. I was fastening my corselet again when I heard a yell and saw Orbius struggling among a group of soldiers. I ran forward to help him and the slinger must have caught me at that moment."

"Your shoulder plate broke the force of the blow. It's a deep wound but I do not think the bone is broken."

"Orbius!"

"The grass is trampled but there is no sign of a body. They may have carried him off with them for ransom."

The youth tried to get to his knees but the effort was too much for him. "I must find my friend," he gasped.

"But where are your horsemen? Why have they not come to look for you?" Zonas glanced round to see if Sikelia had strayed but she was grazing peacefully by the river.

"They are probably pursuing the raiders."

The trader scratched his head. It was a bad wound although not necessarily a dangerous one, still he did not like these slingshot injuries, they seldom healed as well as a clean cut from a knife. The Roman was an officer, his troop might return to search for him and if he helped the boy, they would certainly let him ride with the baggage train, perhaps as far as the coast. "I must get you into shelter," he said firmly, "and then find a messenger to take the news to your camp."

"I believe the peasants betrayed us. It was a sudden attack from the village side."

"You cannot lie out in the sun like this. I can see some huts about three fields away. One of them may be empty or perhaps I can find a man who will hide us if I pay him."

"My name is Karus, son of Livius. We own a farm above the Anio. There should be a couple of coins in a bag at the side of my belt."

"I am Zonas, son of Theodorus. Two Numidians robbed me of most of my goods and left me for dead in the mountains. I am on my way back to Formiae where I have friends."

"If I ever rejoin my companions," Karus murmured, "I will see that you return to your city in safety." He closed his eyes and the voice was so faint that Zonas could hardly hear him. It took him a long time to drag the youth to the river although he moved openly because the Iberians had evidently seized the second Roman and left. "Do not stir," he said, arranging one of the sacks under the soldier's head, "I am going to look for help and for traces of your friend. There is a bowl of water beside you and I shall return as soon as possible. Till then, I will leave my donkey here as hostage."

The Roman was right, the trader thought, as he picked his way warily along the bank. The peasants were selling their produce to the Carthaginians just as they had done at the village where Dasius had left him and his only hope was to find some old man who would not tell the headman so as to keep whatever reward they offered him for himself. He doubted that the enemy was still in the village, it was too far north for them to risk being found in daylight but they certainly had friends there and might return in the evening. He walked on uneasily with a stick over his shoulder, hoping that any Iberians still hiding in the bushes would take him for a peasant about to dig his fields. He had tramped perhaps twenty sling shots when he reached a woman pecking at the earth with a broken hoe. She had the resigned look on her face of Sikelia at harness time without the occasional burst of wild gaiety that the donkey sometimes expressed through her hooves. "Do not be afraid," the trader shouted, being careful to stand some distance away, "I am unarmed and mean you no harm."

All the same, the woman looked up, screamed and would have bolted if he had not run forward and caught her by the arm. "I am a farmer like yourself," Zonas said and from sheer habit of listening to her husband's masterful orders, she stood facing him, trembling but still.

"I am not going to hurt you," Zonas said, giving her a little shake all the same, "I found a wounded Roman by the river and need your help."

"Help! What help can I give?" the woman asked bitterly, "they took my husband for the army and left me to dig the field alone."

"The gods are merciful to those who are compassionate," the trader answered. Fortune must be protecting him or he would not have found the woman so soon.

"I am too poor. Go on to the village."

"Up that hill?" Zonas pointed to the houses that were an hour's climb above them. "The man cannot walk. He is an officer and will give you a reward."

"But the Carthaginians will kill me if they find him in my hut."

"Are they about? The officer thinks that he was hit by some stray slinger."

"I saw horsemen yesterday. They were a long way off and may have been Roman."

"Yes, that was the officer's troop. If there were any Carthaginians in the neighborhood they have fled." Zonas doubted if the statement were true but he had to reassure the woman.

"The soldiers rob us wherever they have been born. My husband had to leave this field and sell our best goat to buy himself a cloak."

"But if you help my master, he will buy you a kid." He dared not offer too much or she would rush up to the village and tell the old wives round the fountain what had happened.

"I cannot leave the field before sunset," the woman said uncertainly.

"Once I have got my master under a roof I will dig your ground myself for the rest of the day." It was the labor that Zonas most detested but it was as good a payment at that moment, he supposed, as any other. A light came into the woman's eyes and he knew that he had won. "Is he badly wounded?" she asked.

"He will not die but he has a fever."

"You can put him in the barn," she still spoke reluctantly, "our other two goats are up the hills at pasture."

Zonas released her arm and bowed as if she were verily a Roman matron with twenty slaves at her command. "If you will come with me, we can bring him here on my donkey. It is better that the villagers do not see us. Otherwise, the headman will claim the reward and there will be nobody to dig your field. In a couple of days I ought to be able to take him on to his camp."

The heat had drawn the moisture out of every living thing. It was the more oppressive because it had come so suddenly. There was nothing but a patch worn bare of grass in front of the hut and the air smelt of dust. Karus lifted the bowl that Zonas had wrapped round with wet rushes but the water was flat and warm. He longed to be lying near the stream below his home where the small pebbles under its crystal surface were banded with the same irregular patterns as the family grass snake that lived above them in the ferns. He was still drowsy from a drink that the trader had given him and he wondered hazily when Zonas would return? Would he have news of Orbius? The loss of his friend was worse than the pain of his wound although this was sharp enough. How could a friendship that had been so complete that, like twins, they had shared each other's thoughts, be broken off in a second? Zonas had found no signs of a body but he had seen hoof prints. "They have carried him off," he had declared. Karus struck the floor with the fist of his good arm. He must help . . . he must help . . . would his mother sell their one fine vineyard? Orbius was a younger son, his own family had little land

and they would not be able to collect the ransom money alone.

Karus moved dangerously near the door, hoping for more air although the trader's last words had been, "you must not let anyone see you." How could he persuade his mother that the safety of Orbius was much more important than the vines? She had changed so much during the last years. How gay and affectionate she had been when she had lifted him up as a baby to hear the owls or joined him in his boyhood to go rambling in the hills. When had her thrift turned into mere meanness? When she said, "I suppose we must let them have a sheep for the Lupercalia," there was always a harshness in her voice. She was just as reverent as the country people whose customs she seemingly despised but now there was no warmth about the offerings and she stayed in her room throughout the festivals with never an extra gift nor gracious word. As for her warning not to joke with the slave girls, how could she imagine that he would want to touch such creatures in their dreary, homespun clothes? He barely knew them by name. He knew that times were hard, that his father had left obligations at his death and that the taxes were merciless but must she always measure the bin to the last cup or tell him incessantly, "I am doing this for you, Karus, when you come of age the estate must be free from debt."

"Yes, Domina Sybilla, no, Domina Sybilla," what had he known of generosity or warmth until his uncle had taken him to join the army? Even then the camp had been lonely until he had met Orbius. Oh, he smacked the floor again in exasperation, why had they posted no guards? Where was his friend? They had planned to live in

Rome together after the war, to study philosophy perhaps or talk. Their minds had been as full of speculations as a tub with grapes and they would never have fallen into that ambush if they had not tried desperately to snatch a moment alone.

Karus shifted his position to try to ease his arm and wondered if the trader would be long. He liked the man although he wished that he did not smell so strongly of onions and stale oil when he leaned over him to dress his shoulder. It was maddening to have to lie helplessly here. He knew that he ought not to have urged Zonas to go up to the village against his judgment but how otherwise would they get news? He tried to fill the cup again from the bowl of stale water when a frightened figure came panting through the doorway.

"We must leave at once."

"Leave?" Karus realized that he had really been waiting for the sleep that followed one of the trader's syrupy draughts.

"The village is full of Carthaginians. If I had gone all the way up you would never have seen me again but I met an old shepherd by a fountain and he warned me. Your ambush was no accident. The slingers had planned it carefully so as to lure your soldiers down the valley."

"And the place seemed so friendly," Karus said bitterly, "we stopped for a night in the headman's own field and he thanked us for protecting him."

"What can they do?" Zonas shrugged his shoulders. "They lose their flocks unless they obey the soldiers whatever badges these wear. Still, I have some news. Your friend is a prisoner but they have taken him inland. Some of your men seem to have got away because the shepherd saw them riding past with a led horse. They will have gone to warn your camp."

"Take me to their officer, I shall surrender to the Carthaginians, I must rejoin my friend."

"I am not going to be sold as a slave by them if I can help it," Zonas answered indignantly, it was so like a Roman to forget that he had been nursed day and night for five days while the trader had lost his chance of getting to Frusino, "besides, they are on the move, a prisoner would be troublesome and they would probably kill you at once. If you want to help your friend, the sooner we get to your commander the better. Do you think you are strong enough to sit on my donkey?"

Zonas did not wait for a reply but hurried out to fetch Sikelia. At this moment the soldiers would be eating their evening meal and from the hillside he had noticed a wood some distance away that could shelter them for the night. He thrust their few belongings into a sack, gave Karus the last cup of the liquid that was simmering over a small fire and put a few coins in the corner. "No, no," he protested as Karus would have added another handful, "I gave the woman a piece of silver as you said the first day and I have dug half her field. If she thinks you are rich she will go straight to the Carthaginians for the sake of the reward but as it is, she may keep her mouth shut, so as to keep the money she has. Let the donkey pick its way, I have the leading rein in my hand. According to the shepherd, we should reach your camp in a couple of days."

"Take the boy to his home," the physician had said impatiently, "he won't be able to hold a rein for another two months." The words rang in the trader's ears as he climbed the slope between the oaks and chestnuts. He was glad of their shade after the heat of the plain. They had been lucky, they had reached a Roman outpost a day after leaving the valley but then Karus had almost died from a lingering fever that the physician had ascribed to a piece of grit in the wound but that Zonas thought was due to the youth's grief for his friend. His commander had refused to talk of ransom till the summer campaign was over. Karus had ridden here on Sikelia because he could not mount a horse but the jolting and discomforts of the journey had brought on his fever again and the trader had left him at a farm in the valley while he took the news to the youth's home. There was no question of sending a messenger. The boys and the few men left on the estate were out cutting the hay.

Zonas trod on a bright yellow leaf that was still sticking to the soil from the last year's gales. He could see the walls of a tiny village high above him through the trees. An acorn or two that the pigs or the children had missed, slid from under his sandals and he noticed with delight the print of a mule's hoof in the dust. Here and there, a number of small white stones had been forced into the sandy earth to form a path. He slapped his hat across a tree trunk to free it from dust and then, hearing voices, dived into the waist high, scented bracken. He did not want to be stopped and questioned because if he were first at the villa, surely they would give him some reward? Two children passed, chattering together, they had been out gathering sticks. He waited until they turned the corner and then scrambled up again until he caught sight of a red tiled roof. There was a row of vines, clinging to the posts almost as if they were bowing to each other, and a patch of white pebbles dovetailed together to form an entrance. He pulled two rosemary bushes slightly apart to peer through their twigs. A girl was standing on a stone step. Her light brown hair was caught back with a ribbon and her face, though sunburnt, was lighter in color than those of the peasant children. She must be a Gaulish slave and if so, Karus was richer than he had thought. He scratched his ear and wondered how much they would give him for helping the youth to return? "Bring me another basket, Verna," a stern voice commanded. The girl put her hand on the rim of a tall, earthenware jar, looked round almost as if she were expecting someone and disappeared into the house. Zonas stole through the opening in the hedge. He found himself face to face with a matron dressed in homespun exactly like the country people but with such an air of authority that he knew that she must be Domina Sybilla. "Verna!" She called again, dropping another rosemary clipping on the pile at her feet. Then she heard the scratch of hobnails on the pavement and looked up. "Oh!" She stifled a scream as she saw what she described afterwards as "a barbarian staring at me with a head like a prickly chestnut husk" but she snatched up her pruning knife and faced the intruder courageously, "what do you want here?" she asked.

"It is your son, my lady," in his excitement Zonas forgot to show the ring that Karus had given him as a token, "he is lying wounded in the farm in the valley and is asking for you."

CHAPTER 7

To be free, to be able to walk at will to the river as a right, this was the only thing that mattered. Verna hid herself behind the hedge, not to be seen gave her an illusion of liberty. She would rather exist in a hovel beside the reeds without a drop of oil to put on her winter beans but with the status of a freedwoman than live on the dishes prepared for Domina Sybilla herself, dressed in the tunics that her mistress might have given a daughter. She knew that Sybilla was as kind to her as the mother she had lost when a baby but this did not make up for the fact that she could not run out to the terrace and say on a spring morning, "I'll go out to the barn and see if the swallows have come back" without asking permission. It was freedom that she wanted, not affection, not even the kiss that her mistress had once given her when she had found a ring that had been lost in the grass. She wanted to be part of the wind and water now while she was young, not when she was old like Utila and too breathless to climb the hills.

"Verna!" Her mistress, of course, had discovered her hiding place. "Dreaming again when there is so much to do! Take this milk up to my son and stay with him while he drinks it."

Verna nodded submissively, although it was hard to keep the insolence she felt out of her face. What right had Domina Sybilla to shout at her? She did not even look like a matron, standing there in a peasant's old apron with shears dangling from her waist. Besides, she would never forgive her for sending Melania away. All Sybilla did was criticize; "wipe the dust from your sandals before you come into the room. Never listen to gossip. A Roman girl smiles, she does not laugh." Melania had been friendly and kind, whispering about the births, deaths and upsets of the farm when they had sat next to each other in the spinning room until she had felt part of its larger, less restricted life. Now she could hardly bear to greet her friend if they met. Domina Sybilla had sent Melania to live with Zonas, that greedy, vulgar peddler, in a hut near the stables. "He needs a woman to look after him," her mistress had said to Karus, "and they like each other. I saw him kissing her the other day behind the fountain. And she is just the right age to have children." Sybilla naturally wanted to keep the man on the farm when so many of the herdsmen were in the army but there were plenty of other girls. She knew instinctively that Melania had been chosen so that she would be separated from her friend.

It was a hot July day, there was no shade on the mountains, the shepherds said that they could hear the grass sizzling if they went beyond the caves where they sheltered at noon. She resented having to carry the milk to a haughty Roman who barely greeted her if they happened to meet in the garden. There he was, lying beside the fountain and running his hand idly over the moss at the side, the owner of the villa who could even order his mother to sell her if he chose and to whom Utila or a mule boy (though she knew that she wronged him when she thought this) were of less importance than a brace of hunting dogs.

"Domina Sybilla told me to bring you this." She put a little stool beside him and as she stooped to see that the bowl of milk was level, something in the line of her neck that was only slightly sunburnt because it was usually sheltered by her hair, reminded Karus of his friend. It was the same movement that Orbius made, polishing a shield.

"Does my mother think I am still a child?" he asked irritably.

"It was the message she gave me."

The hostility in her tone amused him. Most of his mother's women giggled if he spoke to them. A red butterfly with a white eye on its wing, like the one that they painted on a ship, hovered over the flowers. High up, to the left of the villa, a zigzag path entered the woods. It wound between two huts that he could not see but whose shape was as familiar as his home because he had passed them by so frequently. The trees were dense, green and full of thick leaves, the foliage distorted the air so that it hung round them in eddies until these were disturbed by the evening breeze. The white path emerged again beyond the upper farm that also belonged to the estate and where a broken piece of earthenware that nobody had troubled to pick up, had lain for days in the middle of the road.

It was so familiar that he wondered why he thought about it. The patterns were those that he had always known, circles, a spike, an arch. It was a landscape that merged into his boyhood until he forgot, sometimes for hours at a time, the slinger behind the reeds and that shameful ambush that was more painful when he remembered it than his shoulder.

"You need not stay."

"Domina Sybilla told me to wait and take back the bowl."

"And of course you always obey her?"

He could see how much the words startled her but Verna replied with an aloofness that she must have learned from his mother, "I am a slave."

"And you want to be free?"

"Yes." To her surprise, she had no feeling of deference towards this stranger.

"Yet you are dressed like a freedwoman and we all have our duties." The thought of having to endure the hardships of a second campaign without having Orbius to laugh with him was intolerable. "I want to ransom my friend but I cannot find out where he is."

"And Domina Sybilla is anxious about the barley."

They laughed; the girl had a pleasant voice, Karus noticed, no doubt due to her training. It had not the coarse quality of a peasant's shout across a field. "Liberty would make less difference than you think," he teased, he was still unable to hunt and he enjoyed having a companion.

"It would to me. I should feel part of the wind."

It was not the reply that he had expected to hear and it amused him. Verna was like a very young Orbius.

"And what would you do with the wind?"

"Your tutor, Marcus, told us about an island in the west where even the servants were free."

"Marcus! Oh, he was crazy. Still it was much easier to slip away from him when I wanted to hunt than from his successor."

"I liked him. I was sorry when he died. He told us stories in the winter although Domina Sybilla thought it was a waste of time."

It was hardly a conversation that Sybilla would have encouraged but because he wondered constantly if Orbius were walking up and down a prison yard like a trapped dog, he felt sorry for Verna. "But your mistress treats you well, she does not have you beaten."

"No," Verna rinsed the bowl out slowly with water from the fountain.

"Stop with me for a moment, till my shoulder heals, I cannot even pull out the weeds."

"Domina Sybilla is waiting for me."

The girl spoke as stiffly as if she were on some parade ground, his mother was making her into a replica of herself. Destiny was capricious; the villa was living in the past, this trivial action was right, that, equally unimportant, was wrong. Yet a day's journey away there was hardly a blade of grass left on fields where the armies had camped and fought. It was Orbius who had opened up the world for him and made him realize that it was wiser to chase thoughts than wolves.

"I am sorry your friend is a prisoner."

He looked up at Verna's face. He had often seen her

as a child but after his absence he hardly recognized her. She had understood through her servitude whereas all his mother talked about was land. "Sit down," he said again but she shook her head shyly, picked up the stool and ran back towards the house.

"She's gone to that fountain again." The cook dropped a handful of beans into the pail. The women were sitting on the terrace, slicing them up to salt for the winter.

"I wonder what the mistress makes of it?"

"She seems to have noticed nothing as yet."

"Perhaps she has willed herself not to notice. After all, Verna is the master's slave, he didn't even have to buy her."

"If he had, after the way she has been trained, it would have cost him a farm."

"She was too proud to speak to us," the cook wiped her hands on her apron and re-tied a once red ribbon round a strand of dark hair, "when she finds out, the mistress will have her beaten."

"She would never do that," Melania felt differently towards Domina Sybilla now that she had been allowed to join Zonas with time to clean the hut and cook his meals, and she did not want anything unpleasant to happen. "After all, Verna only sits and talks to him. He's lonely and it takes his mind off his friend. I heard him tell his mother that he wanted to sell the lower vineyard to pay the ransom."

"Heard! We all heard. They were screaming at each other."

"It was his uncle stopped the matter. He said that they must wait and find out first where the friend was."

The first pail was full. Melania got up to take it over

to the store room. It was true that her mistress had spoiled Verna but she had also been too strict; the girl had been unhappy. What a disaster it would be if she were banished to the slaves' quarters after having been brought up like a daughter of the house. Ought she to warn the child about the gossip? She took the longer path on the right because it went by a gap in the bushes where she could look down at the garden. Verna was sitting on a stone wall and Karus was talking to her. They might have been two boys resting after a day in the hills. It would be wiser if Verna helped with the beans but she dared not interrupt the conversation. Besides, she knew that the girl disliked Zonas and avoided her: all she noticed was the trader's greasy hands and rough voice. She did not understand how thoughtful he could be even to a slave nor his gentleness with animals. Perhaps Karus would leave and everything would be quiet again; anyhow, for the sake of her own happiness, it was better not to interfere.

In half an hour the sun would set. Was that green oblong of sky above the valley chasing the clouds or was it the other way about? Men knew so little about the secrets of the earth. Detachment was for the old, this was the only point where he disagreed with Orbius, now, exactly as if he were a child, Karus felt that he could never crowd enough into a single moment. He wanted to unite the sound of water and the scent of trodden bracken into some act that would testify his faith in life. He saw a movement on the steep path that led to the vines. "Verna," he called, "what are you doing in the garden?"

She came towards him, carrying the mat upon which

he had slept at noon. He had forgotten to bring it back to the house with him. "I suppose you asked my mother's permission," he teased.

"Domina Sybilla is at the upper farm."

"Yes, I forgot." She had gone there for two days to put her seal on the sacks of corn and the pots of honey. "Surely you can spare me a moment, it's lonely."

She dropped the mat on the ground and stood stiffly in front of him.

"No, it is not an order. I want you to look at the sky, it's still too light to go in and sleep. Have you never felt, Verna, that there are two ways of living?"

"Yes," she looked up with a flash of hope on her face, "there are the free and there are slaves." As Melania had often said in the kitchen those who were born to liberty as their right never understood the difference.

"No, I do not mean that," he was trying to put his philosophical concepts into a form that she could understand, "I mean that life is more than sowing and shearing and that if we could hold the moments when we feel this, we should be nearer the gods."

"Oh, yes, I have felt that up the hills." Domina Sybilla had been aware of it as well on that day they had tramped to the distant sheepfold over the spring grass. Yet what use would his citizenship be to Karus if they did not finish the ordinary work at the villa? They had to pick the grapes and protect the lambs from the wolves. "I should know it every day if I were free, even if I were very old."

"It's a crime to speak of age at midsummer. Come with me, I dropped a stylus beside the stream this morning and you can help me find it."

"It is almost dark."

It amused Karus to watch the conflict on Verna's face.

She wanted to be with him but Domina Sybilla allowed none of the female slaves, not even old Utila, to be outside the house after dusk.

"It will only take a few moments."

"You know your mother's orders."

He crushed a piece of balm between his fingers and instead of answering, "I am the master here," as he had every right to do, he held the scented leaf under her nostrils.

"I will come with you tomorrow morning."

"The night is better, we shall have more time to get to know each other."

"And then you would go away."

"Who of us knows the future?"

"Verna! Verna! Where are you?" It was not an echo but Melania standing on the terrace with a basket of greens.

"If I gave you your freedom, Verna?"

She still shook her head. He did not mean the words at least not in the sense that she understood them. Yet they were both lonely, both so apart from the everyday affairs of the farm.

"Verna!" The voice was getting desperate and they could hear sandals clattering down the steps. "She will find us in a moment," Karus whispered, as he took the girl's arm, "think about your freedom, come."

He would forget but how could she bear the humiliation of a scolding from Melania, her one time friend? She followed as he raced down the slope, they waded across the stream and scrambled, laughing, up the bank and into the meadow on the far side of the orchard.

CHAPTER 8

The great heat was over but there were no signs yet to remind the people of the turn of the year. The festival had started in the valley, the air was full of sounds, pipes, drums, the cries of children and once, suddenly a stern command from the priest. Karus paced up and down the terrace, wondering what was delaying his mother? His shoulder had healed, he wanted to test his newly won vitality in some game, this strength was as ardent as the sunlight beating on his head and perhaps as pitiless. He even envied Zonas. The Greek had gone to Tibur two days previously to offer the promised sheep in a ceremony at the temple. The trader would have more opportunities there to hear about the campaign than in this isolated district.

How slowly the moments passed! A trickle of water splashed into the almost empty fountain beside the white rose, a lizard ventured to lie for an instant along the top of the wall. It was the heart of the villa, the place that he had promised to show Orbius first, "you can talk of your Stoics without any trumpet call disturbing us" but could it be less than five months since they had first met? It seemed an age.

A small flame rose into the sky, they were almost ready for the sacrifice, he could see the priest's white toga distinctly against the drab shepherd cloaks. Where was his mother? She was never late without cause and the people would be impatient for the rites to be over so that the drinking and dancing could begin. He was about to call her softly when she came out to the terrace in a robe that Quintus had given her. It was long and full, correct in every way for a Roman matron in a city house but the thinness of the linen seemed unsuitable for a walk through the wood and the jostling of the crowds. "Waiting?" she asked, smiling at his impatience and seeing in the eager face the little boy who had often pulled her down the hill in long strides to spend his obol at the first stall.

"They cannot begin the ceremony till we arrive." How old she was getting, it was less the wrinkles, although she was facing him in the sunlight without her old straw hat and with her hair correctly piled on the top of her head and fastened with a dolphin headed pin, than the expression on the face itself. She looked as if she were struggling with some inner disappointment. Yet he was here, well again and with no army duties before him till the spring and the crops had been good. "Besides," he continued, feeling that she had noticed that he was staring at her, "it is pleasanter at the beginning of the afternoon before the air reeks of goat flesh and wine."

"Go in peace and if you happen to find a mulberry root among the booths, buy it and give an urchin an obol to bring it up to me before it wilts in the heat. A frost killed our tree two winters ago."

"You are not coming with me?" Karus stared in amazement, "the people will be expecting you." She had always treated the ceremony as a duty. He had been so small the first time that she had carried him home and he had smeared her face with honey.

"You are their master now. The smells and noises give me a headache so, as you are here, I shall keep the holiday among my roses." She pruned and watered the bushes, she thought ironically, but seldom had time to look at them when they were in flower. "Actually," she added, "I did not go last year."

Karus hesitated. His mother was not a woman to have headaches without real cause and he knew that she would accompany him if he urged her. Yet a thought flickered through his mind that if he were alone he would be free, he would not have to escort her from farmer to farmer as if he were his uncle Quintus nor bring her back to the villa when she was tired. "Go," his mother repeated, smiling at him as she spoke, "Melania is helping to cook the kid and will see you get a good portion."

"But you . . . ?"

"My old Utila will be glad of the chance to cook my supper. I shall keep the festival in my own way, looking at the flowers."

Karus still did not move. He wanted to join in the songs, to stamp and run and show the world that he was alive. Why must his duty hover like a shadow beside his happiness? He knew that he had no right to leave his mother alone on such an evening.

"Go." This time the voice was almost angry. "Verna is waiting for you, she left here an hour ago."

"I will try and find you the mulberry." His voice was colder and more abrupt than he intended.

It had to be, Sybilla thought, as she watched him run down the shady path beneath the chestnuts. Only last summer Verna had refused to join the other servants. "Let me stay with you, my lady," she had begged although it was one of the three days in the year when the harshest master gave his slaves a holiday. She had gone instead to a meadow in the hills where it would have been unsuitable at any other time for a girl to wander alone and had returned with a bunch of mountain cyclamen that she knew her mistress loved. "Sit here with me," Sybilla had commanded when Verna had brought out the supper and, trembling with the honor, the child had sat at her feet until the moon had risen. "See, it is as dark as the markings on the iris," she had said to the girl, pointing at the sky, "but nothing in this garden resembles the stars." She had blamed herself afterwards for being too fanciful but they had been as happy together in the soft evening air as if they had been mother and daughter.

There had been no question today of Verna remaining at the villa. She had asked if she might leave with Melania but only with her lips. Sybilla had guessed from the look on the girl's face that if she had refused, Verna would have run away and taken her beating afterwards. She did not blame her for falling in love with her son but for forgetting to efface herself in spite of her training. "Let Karus alone," Quintus had advised, "he has been very ill and needs distraction. Be thankful that he has not sold a farm to buy some pampered Syrian." She had prayed for his safe return for months and now, when he wanted something as he had once wanted a toy, the detachment of which she was so proud changed into hatred. Why did it have to be Verna? She had brought her up from babyhood and once Karus was tired of her, the girl, she supposed, might have to be sold.

There were stalls along one side of the field, children dragged babies behind them little smaller than themselves, peddlers yelled and an old shepherd walked slowly towards the altar with a kid slung over one shoulder. The biggest group was still assembled round the fire where, now that the prayers were over and the crops blessed, all but the priest's share of the meat was sizzling above the embers. Karus walked between the rows, a member of the throng for this one day as he had been in early boyhood, refusing a cake with a joke, accepting a leaf of berries from Utila's friend and smacking a dusty black donkey with his palm as it nibbled a lettuce hanging over the edge of a stall because it reminded him of Zonas. He wanted to find the mulberry seedling for his mother and some trinket for Verna but could discover neither the one nor the other among the trays. So many men had been killed or were in the army, so many others had died from sickness, that even the children could not be spared to pick reeds to make the little baskets for which the valley was famous, the few strings of wooden beads were badly matched and unpolished and the dye had run on a dozen ribbons that a dirty looking fellow had tied to a stick above his pots. Where was Verna, he wondered impatiently? Surely she could have come to meet him? The rest of the servants were standing together, waiting for the distribution of the harvest cake.

A woman nodded and he stepped back to let her pass, one shoulder was pulled lower than the other under the weight of a bale of fleeces. He knew her face but could not remember her name, only that she came from the opposite hill and that she and her husband had once sheltered Mocco and himself during a storm. "I am not afraid of the Carthaginians," the shepherd had said in reply to some question, "what we fear are the wolves. They come howling round the sheepfold in winter, particularly when there is snow."

There was a burst of laughter. A herdsman was telling a story, his knee bent and his arm raised in mimicry of the tax collector at Vicus. It was not a good imitation because the man looked more like some old wooden statue buried under ivy than an official but it was enough to amuse his companions. Where was that girl? He looked up and down the meadow but it was hard to distinguish a single figure among the throngs. It was not until he walked as far as the bridge that he found her, plaiting and unplaiting a couple of rushes. "I have been looking for you everywhere," he said crossly, "my mother told me that you were with Melania."

"She did not want me to come."

"But this is a holiday for everyone."

"She does not like us to be together."

"But, Verna, what foolishness!" He thought resentfully all the same that he could not take the girl alone into the woods that night like one of the young shepherds.

"You are a Roman officer. She wants you to make a good marriage."

"That is for me to decide." Why were they all trying

to spoil his day, this wonderful day when he had thrown a dart with either arm exactly as if no slingers had existed?

"I sometimes think," Verna murmured as if she had read his thoughts, "that all Domina Sybilla truly loves is land."

"She has enough to do looking after what we have." A marriage might bring them farms but such duties were a long way off and it irritated him to have to defend his mother to her own servant. "She wants a mulberry seedling and I can't find one anywhere. Come and help me look for it."

People were sitting on the grass, talking to friends whom they met perhaps once a year. There was less gaiety than usual, the younger men were anxious about the levies and the war, they stood about in groups, exchanging news. There was not a mulberry to be had but Karus found a new apple seedling and sent it up to the villa with a pot of salve made, the vendor assured him, from nine different mountain plants.

"Your fortune on Fortune's Day!" An Egyptian woman sitting on the grass with a scarlet cloth in front of her, clutched Melania's dress as she passed by. Melania jerked her robe away, took a step forward and then hesitated, "what do you want?" she asked doubtfully, staring at the mirror, a bowl of water and various other objects lying on the shawl.

"What can you offer me, my love?"

The idea of anyone calling Melania a love with its suggestion of wings and swiftness sent Karus into a spasm of silent laughter. "Look," he whispered, knowing that Melania had not seen them, "she is offering the Egyptian a pot of my mother's honey."

The woman lifted the jar into the air as if she could

see through the clay to the substance inside it. "You must have built the hive for a single bee," she said disdainfully, balancing the bowl on the palm of her hand.

"It is a special honey that my mistress keeps for her son," Melania protested. She did not add that she had received it legitimately from Domina Sybilla because there was a tiny crack on one side. Had she not covered it carefully with a little earth?

"Sit down. As you are a servant I will give my dole to Fortune too. It is a gift because you cannot call a jar this size an offering." She thrust it under her cloak all the same with a quick movement of her sunburnt hand.

Karus giggled again as Melania flopped heavily to the ground, looking exactly like a cow disturbed at pasture.

"Hold this." The Egyptian pushed a small object into Melania's fingers, "and do not speak. If you say a word before I have ended the evocation, you will lose the blessing for the year."

Karus watched, half fascinated himself, as the woman poured some water into a bowl and began to chant in what was to him a barbaric tongue. There were strict laws forbidding such itinerant soothsayers in the towns but who was going to interfere with them in isolated villages? After all, Melania would never earn enough to sacrifice at the temple at Tibur so what did it matter if a stolen pot of honey (as he thought) brought her reassurance and a hope of happiness?

A small boy burst away from the other children and ran, shouting towards them. He had a tiny bow in his hand and could really have been one of the Loves if there had not been a charcoal smudge on his cheek and a long rent in his tunic. Two men dashed by, with yells and a clatter of sticks, chasing a pig that had escaped. The Egyptian sat through it all, a yellow handkerchief hanging over her head to shield her neck from the sun, as if she were alone beside a fountain. She looked up at last and said in surprise as if she had never seen Melania before, "why, my lady, you are one of Fortune's children. This year she has doubly blessed you."

"Not till now," Melania interrupted, remembering a scolding the previous day because she had happened to spill a small pitcher of milk.

The woman looked at her sternly. "I have seen Fortune's symbol in my bowl, think of me, my lady, when you are rich." She looked round with glittering eyes, aware of everything about her again, "one little extra coin because you will be happy."

"I am a slave," Melania answered, flustered at being addressed as my lady, "the jar, truly, was all I had." She shook out the folds of her robe to show that it was true.

"But the belt! I see an obol near the strap. Just one more coin to bless me with your luck."

"I forgot." She had tied a coin there to buy herself a harvest cake and fumbled till she found it, wondering if the Egyptian knew that the honey pot was cracked because she could apparently see through clothes. "May Fortune bless you as well," she said, dropping the money into the outstretched hand, "now I must see if those boys are turning the spit, all they do is chatter if there is nobody to watch them."

The woman looked up as Melania hurried away and caught sight of Karus and Verna. "Your luck," she said in a quiet, almost whispering manner as if she were afraid that the Roman would order her away. "She does not believe me," she nodded towards Melania's back, "but the signs never lie."

Karus hesitated. The peasants called all these people Egyptians but the woman's face was not African and they came usually from the harbor towns where many races mingled. She had been quick to notice the bulge at Melania's belt and he decided that she probably came from the waterfront at Neapolis. "Take your chance," he said, pushing Verna forward, "see what the year has in store for you."

"It is not allowed."

"But Fortune, my lady, is above the laws of men."

Verna did not move, she had often heard her mistress scold a slave for trusting the Egyptians. "They only rob you of your obols and play on your ignorance." Yet she could not help wondering as she looked at the face that was watching her with some amusement if Domina Sybilla might be angry because her servants snatched a rag of hope instead of buying the strong sandals or the coat that they could wear throughout the year while they worked for her? She smiled at the woman although she was afraid of her and sat down in front of the shawl. It was an act of independence and a sign that although her mistress might own her, she was free at the festival to have an opinion of her own.

"Sit down beside the girl as well, it will encourage her."

Karus looked round, it was hardly dignified for the master of the villa to squat in front of a pile of acorns. He ought to be upholding the laws. "Nobody will disturb us," the Egyptian said as if she understood his embarrassment, "the priest has begun to divide the meat." She leaned forward, her hand wavering over different items on the cloth. "What shall we take? A stone from a Roman hill for you," she put a black and white striped pebble into his hand, "and a root, I think, for the lady. Here is one that my father brought back from Syria."

The incantation lasted longer than it had with Melania and the words were equally unintelligible. It was probably a dialect, Karus decided, that she had learned from some sailor; it impressed the peasants, no doubt, because they could not understand it. He felt the strangeness himself, the stone grew warm in his hand, it was as if they were asking for a guide when the mist overwhelmed them in the mountains. The woman's eyes were fixed on the bowl, she started, her hand trembled in the middle of a gesture, the chant turned into a primitive wail. She ended with almost inaudible words and flung the water over her shoulder. "A long life, my master," she took the pebble away from him, "you will hear the news you desire."

"My friend will return?" Karus forgot his skepticism and did not notice the triumph in her face.

"The signs do not lie," she repeated, "but you must be patient. It will not happen at once."

"If I can only be sure of seeing him again . . ." The shoulder had healed but there were edges in his mind that only Orbius could pull together. He looked up but there was no eagle in the sky and no sign of a messenger in the throngs round the fire.

"Patience." The woman turned towards Verna whom Karus in his excitement had forgotten. "Fortune has blessed you, my lady, but you were born for summer. Beware of the snow."

Verna smiled and murmured her thanks, then she drew, yes, actually drew Karus away by his belt as if he were merely one of his mother's young shepherd boys. He flung a silver coin into the basket, it was three times as much as the Egyptian had expected and walked towards the center of the field to a chorus of blessings. "Come away," Verna whispered as soon as they were out of earshot, "she frightens me. If you want to consult the omens, go to Tibur. There is a famous soothsayer at the temple."

"It was just because of the festival." What had his mother said to the girl? She was stiff, unlike herself, almost a copy of her mistress. People were happy or ought to be, Orbius was coming back, he tossed a coin for the little boys beside the spit to scramble for the prize and smiled at Mocco who was actually carrying a garland. They moved to let a herdsman pass, he was wiping some hot grease from his coat and yelling angrily at his companion who looked more like a rustic god than a peasant with a kid slung across his back, its hooves looped together, and a pole in his hand. "A ribbon! A brooch!" They were common toys and Verna did not want them but if Karus had slid one into her hand she would have had something to show the other girls or even hold up, a little uneasily, to make Domina Sybilla laugh and earn her forgiveness. Why was she so angry? Her mistress would have Karus till she died. Whatever his promises, she only had the summer.

"Good Fortune!" Melania came towards them with two pieces of meat on big, shallow leaves. "It's tender, I kept it for you but eat it while it's hot."

"Good Fortune!" The people round the fire were eating, drinking and shouting the words at each other but it was mere noise, the freedom of other years had gone (or was it because he was older) and Karus felt that only he and perhaps Melania were truly alive. He hurried impatiently towards the crowd that was forming round the pipes when Verna stopped abruptly, "let us walk back to the river, they are beginning to dance."

"And we will join them."

"No," Verna shook her head, "your mother would not like it."

"I shall do as I choose."

"But you are master of the villa," she walked almost stubbornly in the opposite direction. Karus had an impulse to snatch her arm and drag her into the throng but he knew that she was right; he could have danced with a young Melania and nobody would have given it a thought but Verna had been kept apart and brought up as strictly as a free born Roman. "Even my mother cannot object to our looking again for that mulberry tree she wants so much, but if I am the master you should do what I ask."

"I cannot learn disobedience in a moment." If only she could have laughed, Karus would have joined in and everything would have come right again. She should not have left the villa but she had wanted desperately to share the festival with Karus and now she knew that in spite of his promises of freedom, she was doubly bound; to his mother and to this stranger standing beside her. She looked down at the bridge, trying to find some word that would break his anger. The rushes had turned yellow in the heat but there were no new tassels among their stems. "It's the end of summer," she meant the phrase to be careless but it sounded final, like the end of life.

Karus did not answer. The women had combined to spoil the day, his mother by her jealousy, the girl from fear. The people round him talked of war but they had never seen it. A youth crossed the meadow, he was too far off for Karus to see his face, but something in the way the runner moved, reminded him of Orbius. He knew instantly then what it was he missed; the easy companionship, the tossing back and forth of ideas without having to excuse them, that had been his right in Rome. Even the scene changed as he glanced around. It was no longer the feast day of his boyhood. A child whimpered, another shrieked back angrily, he guessed the harshness behind the bargaining as a man changed some tallies on the ground, the grass around the fire had been trodden bare. "You had better join Melania," he said abruptly, "I am going back to the villa."

He strode up the hill while Verna followed, unnoticed, an increasing number of paces behind him, until they reached the empty garden in front of a silent house.

CHAPTER 9

"Way! Way!" If the people pushed back suddenly against the stalls it was less to help the porters than because they did not want the bowls falling on them that were stacked so precariously on the wicker trays. "One *as,* only one *as!*" a peasant in a torn, gray coat held up a large, leaf-wrapped cheese. "The winter will be long, mother," a peddler thrust a hamper of beans under an old woman's nose. "Honey, the best Tiburnian honey!" A shrill voice rose above the clamping of heavy sandals on the cobbles. Zonas stopped in front of a dozen tiny chariots dangling from a stick, almost as fascinated as the children; each of the horses had a blue or red harness painted on its wooden back and a tiny feather in its headband. This was his day; let those who would, deplore the crowds, the hustling and the shouts. He loved the people, the colors and the scents, the pale straw under the apples, the smell of an opened wine jar, the dark brown or the weaves shading to green of the different baskets. "Tiburnian honey!" The boy's yell sounded as if he would never tire and the trader grinned, muttering to the man beside him, "oh yes, we know, one part mountain on top and two parts underneath from somebody's old hive in a back yard."

"And he ought to be a head on a country fountain," his neighbor replied, pointing to a man with a bent knee and a mouth so wide open that the nose almost disappeared in a mass of wrinkles, who was leaning over to bargain for a pitcher. An elderly woman brushed past them with a bundle of greens under her arm and a small bag of grain clasped tightly in one hand. They would be holding the autumn market now at Formiae and for no reason at all Zonas remembered a crack that ran along the wall above his pallet in the room that he shared there with another trader, a crack that turned into a path whenever he rolled lazily over under his sheepskins on a winter day, the path that meant spring, other bargains, a new and different year. "Tiburnian honey!" The clamor beside the big stalls at the end of the row deadened the shout at last. A fellow carrying a bundle of reeds, accidentally knocked the hat half off his head and as Zonas was straightening it, he found himself in front of a farmer's booth. How strange! He had never noticed before that the strips of dried meat swinging from a pole were like the leather straps hanging from a soldier's corselet. He poked a ham with his finger, stared at the barley jars in front of a row of cheeses, and noted that the grains were firm and dry, it had been a good harvest.

No two markets were ever the same, there was always something to be learned and he hesitated whether he would walk back the way he had come or eat now at a wine shop? At that moment, the cries ceased and as he looked round wondering at the sudden hush, he saw an official in a white toga picking his way among the dropped greens and fallen rubbish on the pavement. "The toll collector," his neighbor whispered and the buyers merely looked at the goods or slipped away along side alleys till he had passed. "They seize our grain and clap their taxes on whatever we need to buy here for our farms."

Zonas turned hurriedly aside and walked through the poorer rows where people had spread a single fleece, a few eggs or a pot of still green acorns on the pavement. It was a clear day but though the sunlight caught the roofs of Rome in the far distance, he hardly glanced at the city but turned to stare instead at a rim of silver light that was actually the sea. He was homesick. He wished that he could have been at Formiae for the festival, he would miss the haggling over the nets and the special *patina* of fish that was served on that one day, sole made with grape sauce instead of onions because it was so delicate a fish.

"I shall never see Formiae again!" Zonas shook his head as if such a movement could fling away the thought. "I shall never see Formiae again!" Why did the words go continually through his mind when, more than anything in his life, he longed to see the boats arranged under their brown and white awnings and run his fingers over the drying nets? Homesickness! What business had a trader with such ideas? Besides, Domina Sybilla had sent him to Tibur not only to sell her fleeces but to find a party going to the coast. He had already discovered two different groups and had chosen the one that would pass by Vicus. It meant waiting another week as one of their number was ill and not yet able to travel but they would be ten in all and well armed. He had been scrupulously honest, he had got a whole denarius more for the skins than Mocco would have done and he had kept nothing back for himself, partly because they had treated him so well and also because Domina Sybilla knew to the last copper coin how much her goods were worth. Could he have offended Fortune again? The fear kept recurring to his mind. Yet he had sacrificed a hen at the temple that morning and it was not customary to offer anything as a rule between the Lupercalia and the traders' own festival in the spring.

"Tiburnian honey!" The cry rang triumphantly out again, the toll collector had gone. "Acorns, new acorns," a small boy thrust a basket eagerly in front of him. A child held up a piece of string stretched level with its ears and chewed it. There was a scent of fresh rosemary as well as a rather sour smell of cut reeds. Zonas strolled back down the main alley but he was so preoccupied with this sudden anxiety that he would never get home that he bumped carelessly into a fellow in a soft, woolen cloak who was bargaining over a halter. The man looked up in surprise, they stared at each other, "you rogue," Zonas yelled, clenching his fists, "you left me to die in those mountains."

"Listen to me," Dasius said in a low, commanding voice, catching the trader's arm in a hold that he did not know before Zonas could strike him. "Listen to me. I will tell you what really happened."

"Rogue! Liar!" People were beginning to stare. Zonas wriggled but somehow a foot caught the back of his leg and he would have fallen backwards had Dasius not held him.

"It's a good halter, you won't find a better this side of Rome," the saddler interrupted, afraid of missing a sale. "It's unlucky to fight at the festival. There is nothing that cannot be settled on a day like this over a pot of wine."

"Our friend is right, you will only anger Fortune for a second time if you hit me," Dasius said quietly without relaxing his grip on the trader's wrist. "Give me your advice about this halter and then come and eat with me, it is long past noon."

"You will never see a bit of leather like this again. Only three *asses* and it is worth five."

"What do you think? You know more about *bridles* than I do," Dasius accented the word slightly as he let the trader go. Zonas glared at them sulkily and rubbed his arm. He would have alarmed the whole market if the Greek had not mentioned Fortune. Something was wrong. He had known it for the last hour. "It's not worth more than an *as*," he said but they would not trap him with a word or two of flattery and he did not pick the halter up.

"An *as*! That's robbery, it's worth five."

"I know where you can get a better." A muleteer learned that it was always safer to buy such things in the hills.

"Here, we will split the difference," Dasius flung down two coins and lifted the strap as if he were the toll collector himself doing some man a favor. "Now, Zonas, come with me. I know a place where they cook a kid in just the way you like it and unless you prefer Tiburnian, they have an excellent Raetian wine."

"Suppose you listen to my story," Dasius said. He had insisted that they eat before they talked, saying that he had been up since dawn. Zonas remembered to wipe his mouth. He noticed that the Greek had finished a whole portion of meat, stewed in the Ostian manner, and had not left lumps of it on the side of his plate as in the days when they had traveled together. They were at a pleasant tavern, not the noisy one full of peasants at the end of the square nor the place near the temple frequented by officials but in a large room facing a garden at the back of the town where the other guests seemed to be the better sort of merchants.

"There would not be a word of truth in it," Zonas snapped, he was still angry in spite of the meal.

"Listen to what I have to say before you judge me." Dasius spoke with a new assurance. It was not arrogance, Zonas had to admit that to himself, it seemed to come from a strange and unfamiliar detachment or happiness.

"Don't tell me you were carried off for ransom." It was a common beggar's story and almost an insult.

"First of all, I admit that I was wrong to speak to that officer about the oil."

"I do not reproach you for that, it was natural for you to try to sell your wares but why did you leave me?"

"I never meant to leave you. I went to collect the animals. You know how troublesome the brown mule was and while I was trying to fix the pack, the officer came up to me again. He asked me if I would go with them to the main camp and promised me another order for oil.

I spoke about you and he assured me that he was leaving twelve soldiers behind for a couple of days and they would see you safely to the cross road for Frusino. It was not until I got back to the village almost a month afterwards that I found out what had happened. I honestly thought you were safe."

"You could have come back and told me yourself."

"It was too late, the rearguard was already passing."

"Without the help of Fortune," a memory of the fat sheep that he had sacrificed flashed through the trader's mind, "the villagers would have killed me or I might have perished on my journey."

Dasius crumbled a pellet of bread as he stared at the angry face in front of him. This unlucky meeting could upset all his plans. Once Zonas felt himself wronged, nothing would get the idea out of his head. The man was a peasant, fit, as he said himself, for breeding mules or peddling a bit of leather along the coast but he would never be a merchant. "I was almost a prisoner," the Greek continued, "they kept me at that camp for days."

"Where you learned a lot of tricks from the soldiers," Zonas looked down at his wrist and rubbed it.

"I did not want to hurt you but I was afraid you would alarm the market. Remember, Zonas, if you try to betray me, when we met you had been selling bridles to the Carthaginians yourself. And what about the stater?" Dasius lifted a fold of his cloak so that it did not touch the floor. An official would know that it was made from pure mountain wool and would be more likely to believe him than this figure in rough homespun, speaking a dialect that it was hard to understand.

"I am living with Romans, they will protect me."

"Oh, Zonas, must we quarrel? We are both Greeks

and have had good days together on the road. May Fortune and Hermes on this day of all days, protect us."

"And now you are on your way back to Formiae?"

"No," Dasius looked at the trader sharply, "I am an honest man and owe Alfius nothing. I sent him back his servant, the mules, and the money for the oil that was his due. The man was to tell him that I had heard of a bargain and had gone after it into the hills. If I do not return, he will suppose I have died there. Whatever coins I have now were earned trading for myself since the slave left. I shall winter somewhere here and decide what to do in the spring. Perhaps, who knows, I shall join Rome."

"I always told you Rome would win in the end."

"Let us part in peace. It is likely that we shall never meet each other again. Remember, if we talk rashly about our trading ventures, it is the tax collector who will take our goods."

He was beaten, Zonas thought sullenly. In spite of his anger and his aching arm, he knew only too well what would happen if they were brought before that arrogant Roman whose mere presence in the market had stopped all sales till he had passed. "There is no justice," he grumbled, "but I agree, it is better not to speak of Carthaginians here or at Formiae. Good weather, safe roads." He gave the trader's salutation as he stood up.

"I never meant to abandon you," Dasius spoke with such intensity that Zonas almost but not quite believed him, "perhaps one day you will forgive me."

CHAPTER 10

Gold, all gold, wherever Zonas looked the oaks, beeches
and poplars turned the valley below him into a pool of
color. A cypress, the line of a trunk ringed with last year's
bark merely accentuated the magnificence. It was his
favorite season: the moment when he should be approaching Formiae with dried meat and a pot or two of
honey strapped firmly to the back of the mule. Then he
would have four months to sleep away the aches of all
his marches and to gossip with his comrades while the
winds howled and the rain washed last year's dust down
the gutters. He opened his hand and looked at his silver
coins, they shone, they were his own but they were cold,
they did not seem the same to the touch as the greasy obols
that he tossed into a cloth bag after a round of desperate

bargaining. It was the road itself that he missed; without it even a silver piece was savorless. It was like eating that papery fish from the middle of the bay without having eggs or a single peppercorn in the sauce. Formiae! He heard the name whenever a leaf rustled but Karus had come with the gift, "stay with my mother till the spring and I will give you this. I must take Pluvius with me and then there will be nobody here who understands cattle." It was foolish to be homesick. He would have food and drink, the work that he preferred, Melania to keep him warm at night and a promise that he might leave with the first party in the spring. Winter was desolate in any place but one morning he would sniff the scents of the first rosemary shoots in the air, a signal to start for the coast. "I'm back, you see!" He could imagine the baker in his heavy apron leaving his oven and coming to the door, the shriek of the old woman at the house where he lodged, "I thought the bandits had killed you!" and best of all, the grin on the innkeeper's face, "choose what you like, Zonas, you are my guest." Even the harbor would seem warmer and friendlier for having been away from it for a year.

He could not complain when they were offering him so much yet it was a sad season and a sad day. A man had come from Tibur with the news that there was talk of an exchange of prisoners and Karus had decided to return to Rome. The gaiety of the villa would go with him. Karus would make a good landlord if he were lucky enough to survive the campaign. He would never know as much nor be as thrifty as Domina Sybilla but the peasants loved him and would not steal more than their due from his crops. Pluvius and a servant were already waiting with the horses in the valley where there were still a few roses among the red leaves. He was sorry for Verna, she would miss her companion although they had seldom been together during the past weeks.

"There will be time to send a messenger from Rome before the snows."

Zonas started, he had not heard Domina Sybilla and her son come out to the upper terrace above the hedge.

"Yes, Mother."

"Do not linger on the way. There are many homeless people in the hills and they seem to make no distinction between the enemy and ourselves."

"That is the reason I am taking Pluvius with me." Karus fingered the buckle of his belt although he knew that it was properly fastened. It would be unendurable to be wounded again on this first stage of a journey back to Orbius and he would be more careful than his mother; she had a habit of wandering with a single servant to look at her goats on the pastures above the woods.

"My uncle has promised to come and see you as soon as they have cut the timber," Karus continued, struggling to find something to say. He knew that she ought not to be left alone with the cares of three farms, he wanted to comfort her but how could he make her understand that it was partly her own severity that was driving him to Rome?

"The harvest was good, it is a pity that you cannot stay to share it with us," Domina Sybilla said. She longed to take the boy by the arm as she had when he was a child and she had wanted to show him something, a squirrel perhaps or a puppy's brown ears just showing above the bracken but whatever she did today would offend him in some way. Much as she loved him, with a part of her mind she wanted him to go before they quarreled again and he hurt her.

"If I can get leave, I will ride here to see you before the spring campaign." Supposing Orbius were released, they could come together and he would show him the valley.

"I shall be waiting." She had always waited, Sybilla thought, for his father, for Karus to return, for the olives to ripen, even for life itself.

"Farewell!" He kissed her hurriedly, it was better for such partings to be swift. He glanced at the path, it was covered with oak leaves so it was really autumn, they were the last to fall, and wondered what the spring held for him and if he, himself, would ever see his home again? Then he turned and it was only as he was passing the ferns beside the fountain that he remembered the girl. "Look after Verna," he shouted, "I do not want her to do rough work." Then he chose the steepest path of all and raced down it to the horses.

"He will be back before next harvest," Zonas wanted to be kind.

Verna was staring at the valley where the poplars bent slightly forward over the stream, gold crested legionaries in a ceremonious salute. "There will be no other summer." She kicked a pebble away from the step.

"Each year has a life of its own. Nothing flowers twice the same way but that does not mean that we are always unhappy."

"Who picks up windfalls after being free of the orchard?"

"He will come back after the campaign, and till then remember the days you had together."

"I have no memories. What was, is past. I know that it has ended."

"Believe me," Zonas put the knife with which he had been scraping a bough into its sheath, "there is a pause, a breathing space, in every season. I am lonely myself. I shall not see my friends this winter."

"Go," Verna said, "you are free."

"Karus asked me to stay here till the spring."

"Go to your friends," the girl said scornfully, "and give that denarius back to Domina Sybilla. There is a better silver in front of you to take with you on your journey," she pointed to the stream.

"I am stopping here to protect you." Verna did not answer and the trader realized that he was facing a grief as implacable as Domina Sybilla's jealousy. Had he lost his wits? Why had he never noticed how alike the two women were, Verna was more Sybilla's daughter than Karus her son. He did not know how to console her. He stood there anxious to leave and yet not seem cruel, suddenly aware of his work stained clothes and dirty, freckled hands. "If I could help you . . ." he started to say but what were they but playthings in the hands of the gods? He missed his own city, he wanted to get away from this spot that was permeated with sadness but the traveling season was past and though he had had the most carefree August that he had ever known, as Verna had said, he could not hold it and once a man was conscious of it, it was over. "He will come back," he tried to speak firmly, "perhaps in the spring."

"With his friend Orbius?"

"No, alone." They both knew that it was a lie but Verna bent her head in a kind of thanks. She walked slowly up the steps into the house, her eyes fixed on the ground, without glancing once at the valley. The trader waited until she was out of sight before he went to the stables. A door needed mending and he wanted to forget the grief and uncertainty of the last week doing some ordinary but difficult task. The army was in winter quarters, Karus could have stayed with the girl for another two months and yet he remembered how he had once dashed out of Formiae himself on a stormy day; sometimes an element set the blood ringing in a man's ears, call it the road or a friend or any name you wished and then there was no peace till he went to look for it, even if it were still February with snow in the air.

Domina Sybilla jerked the lot out together, weeds, dead mint stalks and the roots of an old, white rose tree. The bed must be cleared before the rains and she had neglected the garden shamefully during the past two weeks. She supposed that they were gossiping in the kitchen, "she'll be sorry now that she's driven him to Rome" and the cook squeaking back (how she hated that cook!) "yes, and he might have bought a Greek girl at Tibur and sold a farm to pay for her." Let them talk, she jabbed her weeding stick under a stubborn bit of rock and heaved it to the surface, they thought themselves wise but they did not know Karus, as she, his mother, knew him. It was not the matter of a summer month, the boy had his father's mixture of weakness and tenacity once he got an idea into his head and it was better for him to leave her for Rome than to get so attached to Verna that the girl might obstruct her plans for a later, suitable marriage. She had hoped to have him with her for a few more weeks, the winters were so lonely, but his interests were more important than her feelings. The wall that existed between the peasants and herself had never been due to birth but because they lived in the present and she in the future.

She must check the honey tomorrow before the cook had time to hide even a small jar. They would need all they had during the cold weather. The day after she would walk down to their farm in the valley and ask Sulma, the farmer's wife, to keep Verna for a time; not to work, she would neither disobey her son's order nor give the girl a chance to complain about her treatment but they had to separate, at least for the next months. She could tell Sulma that Verna had been ill and needed a change. If only she had not lost her temper with Karus on that sultry afternoon! Quintus would say that the hot wind irritated even sheep but since when had explaining a cause obliterated its results? A bramble caught her wrist and she tore it quite roughly away, then she straightened herself to look down the path towards the rubbish dump. The earth, an oak leaf and a broken stone were all the same faded brown. Why were the young so foolish? Had she ever been as headstrong at their age? She remembered a night of wild protest after her father had ordered her to marry Livius, she had run into the woods not caring whether she met a boar or not, but they had found her and brought her back. Afterwards she had been obedient though never at peace. Fortunately, Livius had left the management of the estate in her hands while he, like his son, went to the city. It was never easy, wolves got at the flocks; a flood had once washed away half of a newly planted orchard, people, even Karus, interfered with her plans. Next year she would have to train a woman to replace Utila who was getting too old to work. Verna was lost to her and she had not known how much she had depended upon the girl. She, rather than Karus, would miss her most.

Sybilla looked down at the pile of twigs and roots that she had heaped at the side of the border. An autumn ago Verna would have carried them to the dump and swept the path but the girl had deliberately joined the other slaves in the spinning room that morning. Did it really matter if they moved the rock that was damming up the stream or if that jasmine in front of her flowered or not? "I should like to go to Rome too," she heard herself say *aloud* to her own amazement. She looked round guiltily but she was alone, nobody had heard her. Her basket was on the ground with the weeding stick beside it, she snatched them up, sent the carefully piled litter spinning in all directions with a violent kick and walked sternly back into the house.

CHAPTER 11

It was January, the coldest month, but the year had turned towards spring. The slab of ice in the basin was the exact shape of its hollow even to the knob on its left side. There was snow in the air and, broom in hand, Zonas paused to stamp his feet and adjust his coat, before sweeping a scattering of leaves, their gold sides uppermost, into a pile below the fountain. He had missed Formiae less than he had expected. Melania had cooked his food, the harness had been so neglected that there had been plenty of the work that he preferred to fill the days and although he had only seen him twice there had been Dasius to keep him in touch with the world. Dasius! He still did not trust the fellow. Was it really accidental that he had chosen Vicus out of a dozen possible places for his winter quarters? It was true that the inns at Tibur asked Roman prices and Vicus was two days nearer the coast in spring. The Greek had appeared amazed when they had met accidentally at a wine shop and had shouted, "but I thought you were at Formiae" so loudly that the other occupants had turned to look at them. Loneliness had drawn them together and in spite of a mutual uneasiness, he had exchanged a bundle of faggots for a leather strap and a flood of rumors, and this had partly made up for the temporary loss of the innkeeper and his friends.

The valley had been more fortunate than its neighbors. No farms had been plundered. Their real enemies had been the Roman quartermasters who had ridden from village to village seizing stocks and paying the lowest possible prices for them with a few words about the duties of a citizen flung in for bounty as if any man could make a dinner out of a phrase! Domina Sybilla had been prudent. She had left what she considered to be a reasonable contribution in her barns and had scattered the rest of the crops in suitable hiding places among the hills. "I must look after my own people," she said almost with a smile of complicity as she had helped to strap an amphora of oil on Sikelia's back and described a cave that was known only to those at the villa. She had cut the quantity of their food, alas, by a third, but they had eaten regularly if sparsely throughout the season.

Zonas bent down to cut away a brown piece of ivy where somebody had torn a stem carelessly from the wall and he wondered why its veins seemed so much whiter in winter as he pulled a growing leaf over the bare stone?

His hands were numb, he put one inside his coat to warm it, the fact that the rosemary hedge would be a brilliant mass of blue in another three months did not help his tingling joints. It was the monotony of these sluggish days that was so dangerous; the blood was thick and that brought dark and terrifying dreams, the dangers rather than the glories of his journeys, a gnawing question as to what would happen when he grew old? It was lonely outside, he would go to the warmth and company of the animals in the stables, it was nearly time to give them their evening feed. He gave a last whisk of the broom and was about to start for the barn when he heard the sound of footsteps. "Why, Mikkos," he said, amazed that the farmer in the valley should have sent his son to the villa when it was already almost dark, "what are you doing here? I think it is going to snow."

The boy was about twelve years old and with a fleece over his shoulders, he looked like an oversize sheep. "My mother and sister are sick so my father told me to bring Verna back."

"Sick!" The dreadful room with the two dead peasants in it flashed into his mind, "have they spots?"

"Oh, no, it is nothing like that," the boy spoke scornfully as if he knew all about the plague. "It is just our winter sickness, a fever with coughs. The girl has got it too, she sat down on a stone half way up the hill and said she could go no further but with so many ill, there was nobody to nurse her."

"I will fetch Domina Sybilla." He knocked at the kitchen door, Melania opened it as he expected because she usually helped the cook in the afternoon. "It's much too early," she whispered, sometimes she was able to hide a scrap of meat for him, "the old woman's in the store room, slip away before she sees you."

"I want to speak to her," Zonas said loudly, aware that he had a legitimate right to be in the kitchen. "There is sickness at the farm and they have sent Verna back. I expect the farmer is afraid of the responsibility."

"Naturally," Melania answered gravely, "she must be worth six hundred sesterces." She was repeating what Mocco had said, such a sum was as much a fable to her as if she had been asked to count the stars and yet, she thought, as she hurried across the newly washed tiles, Verna had been the slowest spinner of them all and clumsy at the loom.

"Zonas!" The trader turned sharply to find Domina Sybilla standing in the inner doorway and not, as they had supposed, in the larder. "I was looking for you," he said, knowing that she suspected him of being there to look for scraps. "Mikkos is outside. They have got the winter fever at the farm and told him to bring Verna back."

"Is the girl here?"

"She is ill too and could not climb the hill."

"Then why did they send her away?"

Zonas shrugged his shoulders, he did not like the people at the farm, they had let a cow die for want of the right treatment, "the boy says his mother and sister are helpless."

"Fetch her, and send the boy to warm himself at the fire." Domina Sybilla turned away as if she knew that the others were watching her face. It was too soon. She had not expected to see Verna before the spring and then, at least at first, not at the villa. Oh, they had been selfish, Karus as well as the girl, destroying the close relationship of years in a few brutal moments. Now there could only be resentment between Verna and herself.

Zonas strode down the path wondering what changes he would see in Verna? How long had she been away? It must be nine weeks now, no, longer, it must be eleven at least. He suspected that Domina Sybilla would be glad of such an excuse to get the girl back. If the old woman had been wise, she would have sent the girl to the farm as soon as she had noticed her son's interest, it would have saved them all much unnecessary suffering.

The trees were bare and although the leaves had been gathered for various purposes, there were a few here and there lying on the ground. Otherwise the slope was as austere as a matron's face. He passed the big oak and was half way along the next loop before he found Verna sitting stiffly upon a log and so quiet that he wondered if she were alive. "Welcome," he said as softly as he spoke to the beasts on a cold morning, "Mikkos says you are ill."

"They turned me out," the voice was so hoarse that he could hardly hear her.

"Domina Sybilla asked me to fetch you. She stopped to make up a bed." He did not know what the old woman's intentions really were but what mattered now was to get the girl under a roof. He put his arm round her and pulled her gently onto her feet. She would die if she were out much longer with such a fever in the cold.

He wanted to ask a dozen questions, when had the sickness broken out, were many ill, had they been kind to her but all that he could do was to drag her up the hill as quickly and as easily as possible, keeping up meanwhile a meaningless babble of encouragement.

"Five steps more and we shall be round the turn of the path, look, Verna, we have passed the oak, don't stop, Melania is cooking you some barley soup, it will warm you and soothe your chest, see, there is the roof of the barn, we are almost there." The words eased his own anxiety but Verna made no reply, she only paused to cough now and again until at the end of the climb, he was all but carrying her. The darkness had come and with it, the first flakes and as they melted on his bare hands he could not help remembering Melania's words, "the Egyptian told the girl, I heard her, there was danger in the snow."

"Verna!" Domina Sybilla hurried out to meet them. She had intended to remain aloof and hand her over to Utila's care but one glance at the girl's face told her that this was no ordinary fever. "You should have taken the donkey," she said angrily to Zonas, looking about for somebody to blame, then she put her arm round Verna's waist and between them, they lifted her over the threshold.

It was still very cold. Sybilla stepped into deep snow as soon as she left the doorway. She could hardly stand against the mountain wind but it cleared her head after the hours that she had spent beside the smoky brazier in Verna's room. These winter sicknesses were severe and took the old but in a few weeks the girl would be running down the meadows again to see if the new apple tree had flowered. Or would she? Did the slaves think that she was deaf? "If the mistress had not sent her to that farm with the fogs rising round it from the river," they muttered, "the girl would be healthy enough." Would Utila never learn that her whispers were as shrill as a shout? "Oh, it's worse than that," she could imagine the old woman's superstitious head nodding backwards and forwards on her wrinkled neck, "they say they forgot some sacrifice when the place was built and it claims a new victim every year."

Eagle or girl, glowworm or warrior, the end was death, it was only the moment that was unpredictable. It was so certain a conclusion that Sybilla had always found it difficult to mourn. She fulfilled the rites punctually, pouring milk and bringing flowers to the tombs of her parents and her husband, yet she often wondered, half in shame, what such an offering meant to her? What survived was something else, a gesture or a phrase, her father's hand upon her arm on her first visit after her marriage as if he had wanted to excuse himself and show his sympathy for the girlhood that she had lost. Were the dead only shadows? What were those new mysteries of which Karus had heard in Rome? "You are too austere for initiation," he had said jokingly when she had pressed him to speak of them but she suspected that he knew more than he would say. Quintus declared them angrily to be the ruin of a state. All philosophies if she tried to think about them were incomprehensible. One day the mountains seemed about to speak to her, the next morning they were shapeless mounds of earth. It was not Karus, Sybilla thought, thrusting her fingers deeply through the snow until she touched the rim of the stone basin, what the girl had played for was her freedom. "Knucklebones, my dear," she had often said to her mockingly, "mistress or slave, we each have duties. Liberty is merely a word." She had known from Verna's face though not from her lips because the girl never answered her on such occasions, that she might as well have spoken to the wind. Well, perhaps she would free her once the dangers of youth were over and after Utila died. It would be more fitting as she grew old to have a freedwoman as attendant and friend. Besides, there would be more value in the gift if it were withheld to its proper time.

They had cut the fronds in the autumn but the bracken would come back, sorrows would come back and the harassments of everyday. The chill in the air began to pierce her own chest. Suppose the servants were right and she were wrong? "My lady," Utila beckoned to her anxiously from the doorway. She turned and hurried back to Verna's room. The gasping had increased, it ebbed and broke, broke and ebbed like the wind in an empty hole. "Verna, Verna," she bent down wildly over the pallet, "try to breathe deeply, Verna, you cannot leave me. Listen, I am giving you your freedom in the spring, listen, Verna, your freedom. . . ."

But the girl did not answer.

CHAPTER 12

Sybilla shivered in spite of her thick robe and the fleece under her feet. She could not remember when she had felt so ill. The fever had left her but she had no strength to move although she knew that her slaves were robbing her and that the villa was in disorder. She had managed to drag herself as far as the kitchen that morning for the first time in ten days only to find that the larder was empty, the floor unswept and Melania, as she knew, lying in the women's quarters with the winter sickness. "Of course there is no meat," the cook had answered spitefully with a toss of her thick, black hair when questioned about a certain joint sent over from the store room, "we have been carrying broth to you for a week." She had laughed so rudely that Sybilla had ordered her to be whipped. It was less the cook's arrogance, however, than her assumption that such a lie would be believed when all the household knew that for days their mistress had been unable to swallow more than a few drops of milk.

"I am old," Sybilla murmured aloud. She longed to slip from the case of a body that now tormented her, to sleep so that she was never forced to see the dust again on the tiles nor hear the whispers, "careful, the mistress has pains in her joints and that means a scolding for somebody," nor have to count the bundles of straw month by month in the barn. Duty kept her alive and she resented it but who would look after the property for Karus if she died? Quintus only thought about his food. Suppose the boy returned to empty stables and neglected vines? He loved this hill, he loved the land as she had never been able to love it because with Livius away in Rome the farm had been the same sort of burden to her as a load of wood on a shepherd's shoulder. She had had to watch and save and counter the peasants, trick by trick. The length of the struggle had eaten away her forces until as she lay here now, alone and helpless, she was more conscious of the cracked tile in the third row on the roof than of the sky above it that would so soon be full of stars. She wanted Karus desperately, if only he could come bounding across the courtyard for an hour but reason told her that she would never see him again. He would follow the illusion that he called Orbius until his own youth was over. He was looking for an explanation of destiny, of matters that even the priests in the temple did not know, shouting questions that his friend had flung back to him again in slightly different words until he called their companionship liberty when it was partly the war. The legion had forced him to absorb in weeks the experiences that would have come slowly and gradually had he gone to Rome to study like his father. The young men were sent on skirmishes to harden them and Orbius, with a year longer in service, had cared for him like an older brother. It had been a lonely boyhood for Karus on the farm. Not even Verna had held him there. For once Quintus had been right, "leave the boy alone. He is very young. It will not last." She wondered how he had taken the girl's death? Passionately at first but after a day he would withdraw into a detachment that he had inherited from his father. Would he bring another slave with him when he returned or would he buy one at Tibur? It would be easier to bear a stranger's presence (if she were still alive) than to have had to watch him with Verna whose very gestures had been almost her own. She could give Karus her bracelet to sell and thus he could keep the vineyard, the one with the golden ears of wheat that was fastened by a clasp of garnets. She had kept it in pious memory of Livius but now, the thought did not even startle her, her husband's face was a mere shadow, and what need had she of ornament? She had not been "wedded on the harvest field" as the village people called it but to save her father's estates. The marriage had been a formal matter with even less affection than was customary. Was love important, she wondered, her feet growing numb in spite of the fleece, would life have been any different if she had known it? It could not be the feeling of reverence mixed with fear that she had felt for her mother nor the fierce, protective instinct that Karus had aroused in her. Willful Karus! She had known from the beginning that he would leave her.

There was a slight, shuffling noise. It was like Utila

to draw the curtain back so anxiously. "My lady, Zonas says that you have sent for him."

Sybilla nodded, her lips could hardly frame the word "yes" she was so weak, but she must investigate the story about the missing stores.

"I have brought you some hot milk," Utila continued, "you must drink it first but oh, my lady, your hands! I will get you another cloak and light the brazier."

"The cloak only, not the charcoal, the smoke irritates my eyes and starts the cough again." To her surprise, Sybilla found that it was less difficult to swallow the liquid now than on the previous day and a pleasant sensation almost of warmth stole through her veins. "Tell Zonas to come at once," she ordered when the cup was partly finished, "and while he is with me, get your supper."

The trader came awkwardly through the doorway, pushed forward by Utila. He had left his cloak outside and stood shyly in front of her, in a short patched coat. It was the first time that he had ever been inside Sybilla's apartment.

"They told me in the kitchen this morning that there was no more meat. Was the joint brought from the store room yesterday as I ordered or has there been some mistake?"

Zonas hesitated. He had heard about the whipping and like most of the men he felt that the cook had deserved it but he did not want to get anyone into trouble, particularly as he suspected that Melania was also mixed up in the affair. "I have been nursing the beasts, my lady, two horses and my own donkey are sick."

"Tell me the truth, Zonas," the command was a firm one, "if you don't tell me the truth, nobody else will."

Zonas looked up in amazement. He had never previously been accused of such a virtue. Roman and Carthaginian alike had referred to him simply as "the lying rascal" or "that thief with the mules."

"It was taken to the kitchen," he need not confess that he had carried it there himself, "but, my lady, if a rough horse leech may plead for a slave's mistake, there has been much illness in the household and these coughs leave a strange lassitude that cannot be cured with gruel. It may be that the meat, forgive me if this angers you, will strengthen them for the plowing. I heard Mocco say that he hopes to begin the long field next week."

Why was even the trader so frightened, Sybilla wondered, was she always and only a symbol of terror to them? Of course they needed more food, she had forgotten this because nourishment had seemed such a burden to her but Mocco or even Utila should have reminded her, instead of letting the cook take it arrogantly into her own hands. She had known all day that the whipping had been a symbol of defeat. "Rule your household by example and a word," had been her mother's final command. Yet nobody blamed Karus if he lost his temper. He was a man. How angrily he had shouted at her in this room, his foot tapping the mosaic at the very place where the trader was standing now, simply because she had asked him gently if it were wise to take Verna entirely away from her duties? Zonas was watching her, she felt, with a kind of rough gentleness. "Very well," she said thoughtfully after a moment's silence. "I will not speak about the mutton again but see that another joint is taken to the kitchen tomorrow."

Zonas bowed. He did not like the austerity that she enforced but Domina Sybilla was reasonable. She would have made an excellent tribune, he thought, looking at her grave head and the long, thin nose but he was thankful that they were not meeting in the market to discuss a toll. Some lift of the shoulders as he turned to draw the curtain reminded Sybilla of the high rosemary bushes that she had been clipping in the summer and of how frightened she had been to see a stranger step into her private garden. "Do you know, Zonas," she wanted to keep him with her a moment longer, "when you brought my son back last year, I thought you were a Carthaginian soldier."

"I was afraid if I saw the steward first he might think the same or not believe my story."

"You say some horses are sick, what is the matter?"

"I do not know," Zonas shrugged his shoulders, "usually an animal dies or recovers in a matter of days but this is a lingering fever. The plain was like a marsh and full of mist all autumn and afterwards the winter was severe."

"I have lived here since girlhood and I never remember so much snow."

"Besides, there were unburied corpses on the far side of Vicus, hunger and much grief."

"Karus told me that you saw the Carthaginian Commander. What is your opinion? Will they invade us in the spring?"

"That is a question only the gods can answer." Why, she has the pallor of a beast about to die, Zonas thought, noticing the white fingers clutching the bowl for warmth; yes, people could say what they liked, they could snatch their togas away from a mule's flank or sniff their rosemary if they met a herd of goats but man and beast were essentially the same, the only difference was that Sikelia was more loyal. "I had neither robbed nor sought the Carthaginians but they would have killed me if Fortune herself had not shown me mercy. It was chance that I escaped just as it was chance . . ." (but was it, Zonas wondered?) "that I saw your son's arm stretched beyond that boulder."

"Perhaps they will return to their own land. It is years since Trebia."

"No," a wisp of straw had got under his collar but Zonas neither dared to scratch himself nor push his hand down his back to get it out, "they will stay in the south till you have a grandson able to bear arms but I think the north will be free of them. They learnt a lesson in those swamps."

"But the Commander, did he speak to you?" Sybilla had heard the story from her son but she was tired of being continuously alone except for Utila who always looked as if she were about to cry.

"Sikelia made him laugh. She wanted to play with his elephant. He shouted to a centurion, 'let the man take his donkey and go free.' "

"They say he is cruel."

"Oh, my lady, if you saw his army you would know that whoever leads them must be ruthless. After all," there was no harm in flattering a woman about to die, "is he not like yourself? It is sometimes good, as with the mutton, to turn the head but we have a proverb in the market, 'a mule that does what it likes with its load, will have a new master by the end of the journey.' "

There was a pride and vitality in this man whom she would barely have noticed if he had not brought Karus back to her that stirred a memory just under Sybilla's consciousness. She had only once before ordered a slave to be beaten. Mocco had caught Lutella stealing a coin that had rolled along the floor after a freedman from the village had bought a couple of goats. "She is not a thief," Utila had pleaded, "all she wanted was a ribbon for the harvest feast." Even Mocco had spoken on her behalf, "my lady, she may really have thought it was lost, she is just a child." "An ungovernable one," Sybilla remembered her reply, because the girl was disobedient although she had been bred in the villa itself. The men liked her, they admired the red full lips that Sybilla found coarse and the lively way she danced back from the well in spite of the heavy pitcher balanced on her head. That night Karus had started up, crying for a little wooden chariot that he had left in the garden. She could have sent Utila for it but she was wakeful; the moon was shining on the fountain, a harmless grass snake wriggled out of the ferns and because she seldom left her apartment between sunset and sunrise the world seemed new, she was afraid to tread on the slabs of crystal lest she mark them although they were simply the familiar stones that she crossed a dozen times each morning and by the time that she had found the toy that her son had dropped, the chariot was sailing like a boat across the dark green waves of what was actually the hedge. It was while she was picking it up that she had seen Lutella, a bundle under her arm and her sandals in her hand, running down the terrace towards the wood. Just as she had been about to warn the household a boy had come forward from behind a tree and as she looked up now at Zonas who wanted to leave and was scrunching the curtain folds between his fingers, the memory for which she had been searching came clearly into her mind. That boy when he had stopped to kiss

Lutella had had the same shoulders and determined face as the trader. She had recognized him as a freedman's son from a neighboring farm. Some impulse had kept her from loosing the dogs just as another had caused her to sleep late the next morning so that it was nearly noon before Mocco had brought her the news. "Good riddance," she had said, "that girl was a danger to the household" and Mocco had answered quickly, "if you feel that way, my lady, I smell rain in the air and it would be wise to finish picking the grapes." The storm had come with lightning and violent thunder so that by the time that Mocco could ride to the valley, the fugitives had disappeared. "Let them be," she had ordered, "the girl will come back in the winter when she is hungry." She had only half believed the words herself and they had never heard what had become of either Lutella or her lover.

"I am tired of war." Sybilla was now talking at random because she was afraid, not of the future but of her present loneliness. Verna would have comforted her but Karus had chosen the girl and now she was dead.

"It is the nature of brutes to fight and so it is with men," Zonas thrust his hand down his back and extricated the straw. The room was dark and Sybilla did not notice his action.

"Life offers us so little it is amazing that we should cling to it," Sybilla continued as if they were both equals and she a man, lying on neighboring couches at a banquet.

"Or sometimes so much," Zonas answered, had the lady not praised him for his truthfulness? "My father was a sailor and he never came back from his sixth voyage so I fetched and carried and stole my supper sometimes on the waterfront. If the sun shone, I was glad not to be cold, and my stale bread was as tender as a chicken's breast when I was hungry. There was always a ship to watch or a mule to tether." He could not tell her about the tavern where they had mocked the magistrate for ordering a beggar to be whipped just for stealing a mullet because it would be impossible for his mistress to imagine such a place and yet now, if he shut his eyes, he could smell the fish bones and the dirty rushes and hear the jokes.

"Comradeship is like honey, it sweetens life for us," he added wondering what he was doing in this chill, orderly villa? The grit of the road was itching between his toes.

"You are a man."

"There are women, my lady, who feel the same as we do." He did not want to tell her that Melania was one but added, unconsciously wounding Sybilla, "I think Verna understood what I mean."

"Verna! She hardly seemed alive!" Sybilla had even wondered if Verna had regretted her lover's departure. "There was a coldness in her even at midsummer."

Ah, there was always a weakness, Zonas thought, giving his back another hasty scratch. With Sikelia it was her right forefoot, with Domina Sybilla it was jealousy. She could have trained the girl to look after the farms better than that idiot, Quintus, who hardly knew a bridle from a halter. But no, just because her son had wanted a playfellow for, what had it been, ten weeks, she had turned the child out into that unhealthy place in the valley. Still he was not going to upset his mistress by defending Verna when the girl was dead. It might provoke her into questioning Mocco about the oats, and they were all that he could persuade Sikelia to eat. "It is not exactly happiness, my lady, it is a gift from Fortune, a feeling . . ." Zonas stopped, how could he explain to a matron who had never smelt life in her nostrils what it was like to plunge into its flood, its miseries, its horrors and (it was the only word he could think of) its richness?

"That day at Anio . . ."

Zonas looked up in surprise, a faint warmth had come into Sybilla's voice.

"Three fugitives raced up to us from a plundered farm and told us that the armies were fighting along the river. I ordered the cattle to be driven to the mountains and sent the women and children to a charcoal burner's hut. Mocco and a couple of men stayed with me while we buried our valuables under one of the trees. Just then, a boy brought news that there had been a skirmish near Vicus and that there were wounded Romans lying along the river. I was afraid of the battlefield but what could I do but go?"

"It was madness. You might have met the Numidian horse as they retreated."

"I thought of that as we were walking down between the oaks and then, because I knew I might never see it again, the wood itself changed. An empty husk or the skeleton of a leaf seemed more beautiful than any pavement in an atrium, even the ones that I had seen in Rome when my father took me there as a girl. I was frightened and happy at the same moment. Is this what you are trying to tell me?"

"Yes, my lady."

"It was a hot, oppressive day and we were tired by the time we got near Vicus. Then I saw a small, dark soldier lying beside the stream. I thought he was asleep till Mocco showed me the javelin. His skin was the same color as his leather cap and his home was beyond the sea, leagues away in Africa. What force, what madness, had brought him here to die in our valley?"

"You were in terrible danger. The man was a Numidian."

"Yet as I think of it now, it was the one day I was truly alive. We found some Roman wounded and two youths lying unburied who had often come to us at harvest time. I remember an old woman who helped me to lift a Vicus boy out of the water. He was not too badly hurt. She must have been a captive because she could not speak our language properly and she had the amulet round her neck that the Gauls often wear. We worked together all day, not as mistress and slave, but as if we belonged to the same valley and I slept beside her that night with my cloak over both of us for warmth."

"Sometimes danger unites us," Zonas said, it had not been his own experience, Dasius had left him, the peasants had tried to take advantage of his helplessness but he felt that he had misjudged Domina Sybilla. That day had been her sole opportunity to break away from the customs that isolated her as head of the household. "Perhaps Fortune's great gift, my lady, is to be able to drift with our time; it is harsh to be abandoned to the past and bitter to see the future."

"I should like to feel that my life has been of some use," what else was there to wish now? The fever was coming back, she had not even the strength to cry out that it should end. She had ruled, saved, scolded and stinted herself for the land but nobody had brought even a hedge flower to the person imprisoned beneath the stiff belt with its heavy, dangling keys. "You cannot write hope on the tablets of the mind" was a favorite saying of Quintus after he got up from a meal where he had eaten and drunk enough for three although he remained as lean as a bean pole in the process. They were words to him, a reality to her. She could have caught and sold Lutella for eight hundred sesterces and planted a grove of olives with the money for her grandchildren. Why had she watched instead of alarming the household? Was it because she had been jealous of a peasant girl in spite of Karus in his cradle and a husband who might have become a senator? It was absurd, she felt dazed and slipping into a zigzag darkness but the coarse, yellow ribbon on the girl's hair haunted her and as she lost consciousness she saw the trader's head bend anxiously towards her face (he was rubbing her hands and shouting to Utila for help) as she had once seen a boy catch Lutella to him in the moonlight.

It would soon be spring. The sky was bright with stars. Citizens or slaves, most of the household was asleep. Melania yawned, she put another handful of twigs reluctantly into the brazier and scratched her head. Domina Sybilla lingered on but the leech had said that she could never recover and then what would happen to them all? "You had better go to bed," Dasius grumbled, "if that beast of his is really sick, Zonas will stay beside it all night."

"Without a thought for me." It was late, she had cooked for the man as if he had been Hesperus himself although she had only just got up after the fever, she had bullied Arco into giving them his best fleece and now there he was, down at that wretched stable with his cough because eventually he had had the sickness like everybody else, tending that wretched donkey as if it were a girl. She got up slowly, her legs stiff from the cold, to stir the soup in the pot suspended over the charcoal blaze. "I hate winter. The sickness seems to get worse every year. It oppresses the liver . . ." (her eyes filled with tears as she remembered an unmerited scolding from Mocco that morning) "and weakens the chest. That is, if people do not die from it."

"I am sorry Verna died. She would have fetched a good price in Rome if the vines had ever failed." Dasius moved his stool a little nearer to the blaze. He had come up with the lawyer whom Domina Sybilla had summoned from Vicus and if it had not been that he wanted to talk to Zonas, he could have slept inside the villa itself. "You are the best cook in the region," he pleaded, smelling the soup. "Give me just a spoonful to keep out the cold."

"Domina Sybilla does not think so," Melania grumbled, "but is it my fault if her gruel gets cold? She sits with it on her lap instead of eating it."

"The fruits of greatness," Dasius teased. Domina Sybilla had sold the cook and had taken Melania out of the spinning room in her place. "Still, I agree, your former companion has an easier time."

"In a freedman's house with only two slaves!"

"But a lazy wife so the cook does what she likes, away from the old one's eyes."

"I would rather be here." The work was hard but she would never have believed before what a difference it made if the pots were hung in their proper places and the steps were kept clean. "I wish Domina Sybilla would get better. They say the son may be away for years."

"Quintus will inherit the place if the boy does not return."

"Our master will come back but not for some time. The auguries said so, at the summer fair."

"Oh, the auguries!" Dasius shrugged his shoulders.

"If you are impious there will be no soup."

"I meant that not all can read them," he answered hastily. The cold air had made him hungry.

Melania ladled a little broth into the smallest bowl that she could find and as she put it in front of him she thought of the Egyptian woman sitting beside the scarlet cloth on the grass. She even saw herself in front of it, grudging the pot of honey, yet wanting to give it at the same time. "As happy as mortals may be." Naturally she had added that small, extra coin. She was not happy, however, at this moment. No, she was angry with Zonas. He loved that donkey just because it was a symbol of his wandering life and how could she bear it if he took again to the roads?

"Just a spoonful more," Dasius pleaded, pointing to the bowl.

Melania shook her head. She had made the soup for Zonas and had risked a legitimate scolding by hiding the ox bone under her apron. She would not give the fellow another drop, he was constantly urging her companion to join him in some risky venture but if she had not let him have the first helping, he would have complained about her stinginess. What did he want coming to their hearth at this time of night? She wished that he would leave, then she could doze by the fire until Zonas came home.

"I saw one of those blue flowers out in the fields today. I forget its name but it's a sign of spring."

So that was what he wanted! Spring, a new journey, somebody to doctor his mules. She stared blankly into the brazier and imagined the future once her mistress died and Zonas went off to the coast. They would send her back to the spinning room again and eventually she would be sold. Didn't these fools remember that there were deserters from both armies all over the hills and that if they escaped a sling shot, there was plague? "We do not sacrifice enough to the gods," she muttered, stirring the soup so that it would not burn.

Dasius yawned, the woman was tiresome and he would have gone to the stables himself if it had not been so dark. They heard footsteps coming across the yard, a rustle as Zonas shook himself because a light rain was falling and then he came through the doorway in the great cloak that he had bought from Arco, looking exactly like a shepherd. "She's eating," he said, "but what a fright the brute gave me. I thought at sunset she was going to die."

"It takes more than cold to kill a donkey."

"When she came to me, Sikelia was half starved."

"Now you have a mule."

Zonas did not reply. He took a mouthful of soup from the bowl that Melania handed to him and began to cough.

"There!" Melania glared angrily at them both. "Now you have brought your fever on again, sitting in that drafty barn."

"It's only the smoke."

"Smoke!" She flung up her arms in the gesture that she used whenever she was accused of taking too much meal. "Show me what we have to put on the fire, we finished the charcoal yesterday and there's hardly any wood left."

"Peace, Melania," Zonas said hastily, "eat your soup and go to bed. Dasius and I have business to discuss together."

It was worse when it happened than the fear of expecting it to happen. It was final and she was helpless. This might be the last night that he would lie with her and now he would come late and argumentative after too much wine and talk. She looked at him pleadingly but the trader frowned. She had planned to leave him her share of the broth but unless she helped herself, Dasius was greedy and would eat the lot. It was good, she had worked on it for half a day. "Leave us the wine," Zonas ordered directly she had wiped her bowl clean with a piece of stale bread, "you need not stay." She dragged her sheepskin pointedly to the far end of the room, determined to shut her eyes but to listen to their plans. The fleece was warm, she was drowsy after her own attack of the sickness and she fell asleep in spite of herself while they were still discussing the weather.

Dasius leaned forward directly he saw that Melania was not spying on them, "are you ready to join me? I am leaving in two days."

"For Rome?"

"Rome! That Elysium of tax collectors! No, I have found a guide to take us to Apulia."

"It is too late," Zonas filled the wine cups for a second time, "Carthage has lost its chance."

"Courage, Zonas, two days on the road and your cough will vanish. I offer you equal partnership although I have three mules."

The first grass, the sharp scent of the broom were part of his blood but there was also the memory of that dark hovel where he would have died if Sikelia had not chanced to push open the door. "The days have gone," Zonas answered sorrowfully, "when two men can travel alone."

"Oh, it's still too cold for the Numidians to be about, we shall have the guide and you forget my token." Dasius glanced round but Melania was snoring and he held it above the brazier so that the light flickered on the silver horses.

"I do not trust the Carthaginians," the trader pulled a few twigs from under his cloak where he had hidden them and put them one by one on the fire.

"The Africans will win. They will invade the north again in a year or two and sack Rome."

"But they have already marched to the walls and left! No, the Romans will win in the end because it is a people against an army. The Commander's own city is disloyal to him. Have they sent him ships or wheat or troops?"

"Loyalty! What a word to hear from a horse thief!" Dasius laughed and slipped the token back into his bag. "You have been crossing from side to side, you Greek, since you were born."

"We are what Fortune makes us." Zonas refilled the cups but was careful to spill a few drops of wine to the gods before he drank. "Most men think their fellows are tools to be cast aside when worn but until the Messenger comes for me I shall never see a man like Hannibal again." It was the first time that he had dared to say the name aloud.

"Join me and you may see him."

"No," Zonas shook his head, "this spring you must go alone. Good bargains and a short life." It was a joke of the road when they grumbled about hardships.

"Why should it be shorter than your own if you stay here?" the trader's obstinacy was beginning to irritate him and Dasius felt an anger rising that he found diffi-

142

cult to control. "I am not asking you to go to a camp but only to a village where I can sell my oil. Afterwards we can make for the coast."

Zonas rubbed his eyes, he wished his friend would leave and let him sleep. He did not like the Romans but once a man understood their ways and the weight they gave to a word (it was like an oath to them) they could be tricked as easily as a Sard or a Gaul. He smiled, remembering the time when he had sold a dagger to a mercenary simply because it had had a scarlet tassel dangling from the hilt. "It depends on my cough. I must get rid of it before I leave."

If it were a passing sickness it did not matter. Dasius leaned forward to warm his hands over the brazier. He had begun to fear it was an attachment to Melania or even that Zonas was negotiating independently with somebody at Vicus. "I have never known you turn a venture down because you were afraid of it. There are plenty of women as good as she is," he jerked his thumb towards the sleeping figure in the corner, "although I admit that she is an excellent cook. You will have to leave your donkey and bring just the mule but if you like, I will wait for you an extra day."

Leave Sikelia! And forget the soft brown muzzle opening that door? It might have been the smoke or swallowing his last drop of wine too hastily but Zonas choked. "No," he said as soon as he could get his breath, "it is unlucky to postpone a journey unless the omens are bad. Mocco has a balm that cleared his chest in a couple of days and I will ask him for some tomorrow." If they started an argument now they would never get to bed.

It was beginning to be hot. The midday wind had not started to blow. Zonas sat down on an old tree trunk and stared at the valley. Sikelia was resting comfortably in her stall. Melania was busy in the kitchen because Quintus had arrived the previous night and he had some duties himself but these could wait while he watched Dasius reach the river.

There was a cloud here and there to show that it was not yet summer but there were lettuces ready to be picked and many small plants in Domina Sybilla's garden were in bud. It was a pity that she would never see them flower. The physician had said that only an almost inhuman determination to see Quintus had kept her alive till now. Zonas stood up, Dasius ought to be coming into view, yes, there he was, leading the first mule along the river bank where the gold tipped reeds divided water and land. "You are a fool, Dasius," he muttered out loud, "and so am I." What was he doing here with his legs prickling, the markets open and the days still cool? Why had he sent that messenger to Vicus telling his friend that he must spend the season here? His sandals needed mending but he had left his hunting boots to dry in the yard and as he stooped to tie the broken thong he caught sight of an object wedged between two stones, a husk that must have been there all winter but that by some chance still contained a chestnut inside it. It stared at him as fixedly as the Numidian on that hill. Destiny had brought him, the son of a cook and a sailor, to a position beyond his dreams in these remote and lonely hills. There would be wine, Melania, power and his own donkey. Yet if he accepted Domina Sybilla's offer he might never feel a leading rein in his hand nor smell the rosemary again on his native rocks. What did the gods want eventually from man? People fell haphazardly like the pebbles that he was now tossing idly into the center of a broken wine jar and not even the wisest philosopher could explain their destiny. He was no Stoic, he had acquired his rhetoric in the fish market and the stables, wiping his greasy hands on a leather apron, but at least he had learned one lesson. A man had to be ready to take his opportunity. If he failed once it was offered to him, Fortune seldom offered him a second chance.

Zonas took a step forward. Suppose he risked everything on one last journey? Melania would look after the donkey for his sake, he could fetch his traveling cloak and slip away before the lawyer summoned him. There was the track with the ruts, the stone walls and the white daisies, in a hundred years it would be the same, he hesitated, "never tempt the gods twice" was his favorite proverb, he raised his arm slowly and let it drop. He could feel, if he could not see, the disappointment on his friend's face and he did not need to be a soothsayer to know that this time they would not meet again. Partings were common on the road but Zonas flung himself down abruptly beside a bush of overgrown lavender, he resented the sound of the water, the sun on his neck, as if he were already an old and querulous man.

Melania came timidly towards him with a saucer. She had been so sure that he would leave with Dasius that she had ventured to steal a hunk of dried meat for him from the larder. "Is Sikelia better?" she asked, hoping to placate him.

"Yes," that wretched donkey had saved his life again because if Dasius had not suggested leaving her, he might now be walking down the valley. He muttered aloud, not to Melania but to an incurious butterfly, "there

are times when a man doesn't want to be saved."
It would not be too bad a life, he supposed, if he kept
the rules. There would be journeys to Tibur, he could
walk on grass and bargain over sheep but the great
wanderings were over. It was almost time for the lawyer
to summon him, how the man's assumption that the
trader's only sensation must be gratitude had irritated
him on the previous night. "They have offered me the
management of the upper farm and the cattle, Melania,
at least until master Karus returns."

"Oh!" Melania gasped at him like a flustered, flapping
duck astray in a strange yard. To her, it was a great
position.

"Mocco refused it. He said he had enough to do with
the villa and with the wine."

"Tasco is not good with the goats." She had herded
them herself and she knew.

Zonas nodded. He must go as slowly as possible, that
way he would make few enemies. He had had mule
boys so ignorant that they had let their beasts get galled
the first day but instead of beating them he had shown
them how to pack the loads and by the end of the season
they had been as careful as he was himself.

"I would rather have gone with Dasius."

"But . . . if you manage the farm you are almost
a steward." The wind had begun and Melania pushed
the hair back from her eyes. Zonas was here but her
prayers and offerings had been in vain; he would marry
some freedwoman because there was no place in a farm
house for a slave like herself.

A boy came running up, "Domina Sybilla is ready
for you," he said respectfully and Zonas could not resist

a momentary pleasure. Yesterday the urchin would have yelled to him from the terrace.

It was time to put Melania out of her misery. She was looking at him as reproachfully as Sikelia when he put the salve on her forefoot before giving her her feed. "I want a boy with a feeling for mules in his blood, not, as here, where they have to be taught."

Melania did not answer. She knew that she would be sent back to the spinning room directly her mistress died.

"Wash your hands. Domina Sybilla offered me a gift and I asked her for your freedom. She is giving Utila and two of the men their liberty, that is why Quintus and the lawyer are here."

Zonas expected that she would fall on her knees and kiss his hands in gratitude but to his amazement, Melania screamed. "It is just another of your Carthaginian tricks, you will send your children to the road if you don't go back yourself. You are no more a farmer than that eagle."

The trader looked up, he had not noticed the bird, it rose over his right shoulder, a good omen on this decisive morning. "Come," he said, giving Melania a hard clout and a shove as if she were some recalcitrant mule, "we must not keep the mistress waiting. And remember now, you are not to steal meat again, I will buy whatever is necessary."

They walked up to the house, Melania sniveling beside him. The buds were open on the two quinces by the fountain, a fern had rooted in the red bowl below the steps. There was a lot to do, he must find a beam to repair the second stable door and get men to help him remove the tree that had toppled into the stream. Another spring, he thought, another spring . . . it might do him no harm to have a year at pasture. "Thank the gods after the ceremony, and then your mistress. You are not to gossip in the kitchen afterwards until dinner has been served. But," he added because he was generous whenever it was possible and it was a great day for her, "we will make a feast ourselves when we get up to the farm."

CHAPTER 13

"Stand here, if you keep out of our way, you can watch us enter the harbor."

Dasius moved across to the spot that the captain indicated and looked round carefully to be sure that he was not obstructing the crew while they checked the two great anchors lying along the deck. He was too excited himself to do anything but watch the shore. What would it be like, this new country, that he had risked so much to reach? He was friendless there although he had some messages to deliver to their families from officers stationed in Lacinia but these men had been away so long that their relatives might well be dead. "You brought us luck," a sailor said cheerfully as he passed, "we had fair winds all the way and saw no raiders."

The outlines of two big temples began to detach themselves from the hills on which they stood and the reality of everything that Dasius saw about him was more powerful even than the fierce African sun. He felt that he was waking up from a lifetime's dream and that the most ordinary things were utterly new, that great red sail, for instance, tugging at the stays or the seabirds diving for a handful of meal. It must be like the culminating moment of a mystery. All other experiences dropped utterly away. Destiny itself had brought him here and he trembled when he thought of Lacinia. He had drowsed away the time, filling up his days with unimportant tasks, neither happy nor unhappy till a fellow trader had come over to him one evening in a wine shop to bid him farewell. "Take your choice, there is Greece or there is Egypt but I am getting away while there is still time. One day the Commander will have to withdraw to Libya, his troops are getting old, he has lost a lot of them through sickness or in skirmishes and he is too far from Gaul to get many new recruits. Take your choice," the man had repeated, glancing round to see that he was not overheard, "I am sailing for Athens next week."

Dasius pulled the brim of his hat forward to shade his eyes. He had gone to sleep that night with a dozen plans tumbling about in his head to wake next morning with a purpose as clear as the early morning light. He had hurried to the harbor to find Mago, one of the two Carthaginian captains to get through the Roman blockade that summer and had asked him for a passage when he sailed. Mago had hesitated for two days. "It's late in the season, you would have to winter in Carthage and who knows if any boat will attempt to get here next spring." No other trader would have made such a de-

cision but he had pleaded until the captain had agreed
to take him aboard. Now the city was rising before him
in all its beauty, temples, palaces and walls seeming to
move gently in the heat as if they were resting on a
line of ships instead of on the ground. They looked at
such a distance as white as if they were built from shells
with flashes of iridescence the color of a mullet's fin
where here and there the light caught the occasional
green oblongs of a garden. "Carthage, mistress of the
seas," he murmured the phrase, half in homage, half in
greeting. Times would change in spite of the disasters in
Spain and Sicily or Rome's new fleet. If Fortune were
with him and the tolls were not too high, if he could
sell his bales for a good price, if they would give him
permission to stay, he would settle here and eventually
buy a house.

"This is the twelfth time that I have entered the port,"
Mago said, lifting his cap and running his fingers through
his grizzled hair, "but I still feel as amazed as I did when
I was a boy and came home from my first voyage."

Boy! When I was a boy! A memory flashed through
the trader's mind of passing the statue of Hermes the
Wayfarer in a long street at Tarentum and hearing the
name Carthage for the first time. "A sailor told me when
I was a child that the fields of Africa were covered with
gold. I imagined that he meant gold pieces laid edge to
edge and supposed it must be a sacred land or people
would take them away." The Romans had destroyed
Tarentum; this memory and the city in front of him were
now all the citizenship that he possessed.

"I must take you to the desert before you leave. It's
a day's ride inland from the coast."

Dasius glanced up at the lean face beside him that

seemed to have settled into similar lines to the shape of the ship. He was surprised at Mago's sudden friendliness. His future was in the Carthaginian's hands because his trading depended upon the report that Mago would make about him to the officials. Carthage had the reputation of welcoming foreign merchants but as people said until the phrase became meaningless, "times have changed." Apart from a few words about the wind or their course he had been unable to break through the man's reserve, although he had had plenty of leisure during the long voyage to think of the hindrances that might occur and to wonder if he had been wise to pack so many drinking cups into his bales?

"That is Byrsa," Mago pointed towards the shore, "we anchor in the port beyond the entrance you see ahead of us. The naval harbor is the other side and we can't see it properly till we land."

"I was wondering if you could tell me of some quiet inn? The places near a harbor are so noisy."

"All inns are bad," Mago said as if he were giving an order to change their course.

"If I am able to sell my wares, I thought I would try to find a place outside the city."

"Why not spend the winter at my house? It's five hours up the coast but very quiet."

His Carthaginian was good but had he misunderstood a word? "You can't mean that you would accept a stranger in your home?"

"Sailors worry less about foreigners than landsmen. Are we so different from each other except in our special knowledge? You are ignorant about the stars and I should not have known what to put in the bales. What did you decide to bring eventually?"

"Ten jars of Campanian wine, following your advice, so you do know something about it. I filled up with those small Samian drinking cups that were much in demand at Tarentum. Apparently your citizens use them for banquets."

"We make a lot of pottery ourselves but these cups are lighter. I will send a man ashore with you when you land. It will take a few days till the ship is in winter quarters and you will want to sell some of your wares. Then I will come and see you at the inn and if you like, you can travel with me."

"I do not know how to thank you." It would mean protection as well as shelter till the spring.

"One warning. Be careful what you say about conditions in Lacinia. The Commander is not as loved here as he is by his soldiers. Oh, there's the guard ship coming out to summon us," Mago pulled his cap on his forehead and strode over to the steersman to wait for orders.

The anchors splashed. It was hotter now that they were motionless and Dasius felt his new robe clinging damply to his knees that were used to light and air. Only horsemen and slaves wore chitons in Africa and he had been careful to have two garments made for him in Lacinia so that he would not look conspicuous on arrival. It was the first time that he had put on the robe and he noticed with some irritation that its clinging folds obliged him to take short, slow steps as if he were already an old man.

The space round them was full of ships, each in its own berth. The quay was full of people but unlike some Lacinian port where it would have been hard to hear an order above the shouts, the crowd waited silently while the sailors moored the boat. Two or three people lifted a hand in greeting, otherwise the only sound was Mago's voice. The tassels on a Numidian's headcloth fluttered as he moved, they were the same sandy brown as his skin. Both of the Carthaginians in front of him must be officials; bands of red and blue embroidery ran the length of their robes and they wore the emblem of Tanit round their necks on short, gold chains. The throngs of almost naked Ethiopians behind them were certainly dock slaves. The stiff loops of their hair reminded Dasius of the patterns that a porter made casually with his thumb in a block of wet clay. He had sometimes seen an isolated captive at Formiae but never a large group. One of the Carthaginians signed to them and they moved with the powerful ease of some great animal to place a gangplank against the ship.

The scene was different from the places he knew. He noticed that the fishermen had their market at the far end of the quay so that there was no mixing up of nets and bales and that slaves kept sweeping the stones as if it was an entrance to a forum. He would be called for questioning presently but he forgot his fears watching the passers-by and was surprised when Mago sent a sailor to summon him.

The two men standing beside the captain were the Carthaginians whom he had noticed on arrival. "Welcome to Carthage," one of them said, "it is some time since any merchants have reached us from Italy."

"I had to wait for a ship."

"Your name?"

"Dasius, son of Scopus." They must not know that his father was a Roman. "I was a citizen of Tarentum but when the Romans took the city I was buying leather for your forces in the mountains. Naturally I did not return. Here is a letter from your quartermaster at Kroton." He wondered as he handed it over if they would guess that it had cost him a link of silver?

The Carthaginian looked carefully at the seal before he broke it and Dasius was glad now that he had on the robe, it hid his trembling. He knew that they might decide he was a spy, for Fabius Maximus or their own Commander, it did not seem to matter which and in that case, he would be tortured and his goods confiscated. Yet although the interrogation was severe, unlike a Roman, there was no trace of arrogance in the official's voice. "You are recommended to us as an honest dealer," the man said presently as if the trader were unable to read. "Have you been a long time with our army?"

"No, I was traveling among the villages to get supplies. My business was only with your quartermaster."

"When did you see the Commander last?"

"I have only seen him once, two years ago, from the middle of a crowd when he rode back from the sacrifices."

The man looked at him sharply but except that Dasius had added a year, that part of his story was true.

"You speak our language well, it is unusual."

"Oh, not well but I used to talk to your sailors on the wharf at Tarentum when I was a child. It amused them to teach me words."

He noticed that the official glanced at his companion who nodded. "I will see you tomorrow about the tolls after your bales have been unloaded. Meantime you may go ashore. Sleep soundly, we shall be as reasonable as possible with a merchant who has risked so many perils to reach our market."

Dasius bowed and murmured his thanks and then bade Mago a ceremonious farewell. The captain replied with the accepted phrases but his face was impassive and he made no reference to his offer of hospitality. A sailor came forward with a small sack containing the trader's personal belongings and he followed the man gravely, trying to imitate the leisurely gait of the people around him. "May Hermes be blessed," he muttered in his own tongue as he stepped onto the quay.

Now that he was ashore he could see the warehouses along the wharf, each with an armed guard in front of it. A few people shouted questions at his companion but they were about the voyages and the ship's cargo, nobody asked about the Commander or the army. The rumors that they were unpopular in Carthage were evidently true. He suspected that Mago must have said something in his favor or he would have had more difficulties with the officials. Now that they were nearer the fish market he could sniff the familiar smells of brine, wet rope and gutted fish. "All ports have the same smell," he said and the sailor nodded.

They turned to the right, walked up some steps and found themselves in a crowded street. People pushed past, sometimes they stared and suddenly, it might be the reaction after his questioning, Dasius could not suppress his terror. Wherever he looked the faces were dark, from the charcoal heads of the Ethiopians to the farmers whose cheeks were the dull red of a newly cut furrow under the veils that they wore, hanging from their conical caps, to shield their necks from the sun. The robes were white, only a few slaves wore a shorter garment made from a dusty brown wool. It was oppressively hot, he was a stranger in their midst, far from the rivers of Italy, with only Mago's "you can spend the winter at my house" to cling to as if to an anchor.

They reached a square as long as a horsemen's training ground with a temple at the end of it. "If you want to make a thank offering for your safe voyage," the sailor said, "I will take you to the place where we worship. This temple is only for our rulers." Dasius looked at it curiously and saw that there were sentinels in front of the great pillars. Each had a lion sitting beside him, as if a guardian of the city, and each grasped the heavy silver chain that was fastened to the animal's collar, firmly with both hands. Otherwise they stared disdainfully at the roof tops as if the throngs below them were of no more importance than flies.

CHAPTER 14

The color of the landscape was in the sea and sky, a
turquoise that never moved, a blue triumphant arch.
In an hour, the African darkness would obliterate the
wall on which Dasius was sitting but for the moment
the light glittered on its white surface as if the night
had no power over it.

"What are you trying to draw? A chart?"

"No, Mago, just lines. It was to pass the time."

"I know you cannot tell whether a channel is deep
or shallow but if you want to amuse yourself, stick to
knucklebones. Some of our neighbors might denounce
us both if they saw you making those marks. We are
taught to guard our courses with our lives."

"I was your passenger and you could have sailed me

into Syracuse and told me it was Carthage for all I should have known," Dasius ground the pattern out with his heel, "it's this waiting. Are the Romans going to invade us or are they going to leave Africa alone?"

"Invade us! The Roman fleet is afraid of leaving Sicily but unless the City does something about raiders, we may never haul up an anchor again."

"Why don't they send some galleys out to clear the seas? Those wonderful ships you showed me are rotting in the harbor."

"Why? Why? Sailors founded Carthage, the fleets brought her wealth but now all the magistrates think about is Numidia. My steersman came to tell me this morning that he is going to work at the arsenal. I can't blame him, this is the second season that we have not sailed, but if a man stays ashore too long, he loses the feel of the winds."

"It's hard to remember that I have been here two years, and such happy ones. You have treated me like a brother." They now felt each other's moods without the need of words and one reason for his anxiety was that Dasius knew his friend was as uneasy as himself.

"It's only your tales that have kept me alive," Mago took off his cap and brushed away a fleck of dust, "we've lost Sicily, we've lost Spain and most of the men I sailed with when I was a boy, are dead or slaves."

Dasius glanced down at the scuffed sand in front of him and cursed his thoughtlessness. He had tried with his whole mind to adapt himself to Carthaginian ways. He had bought and sold for the villagers, using his experience to get them a better price for their wares, he had learnt to prune Mago's vineyard and keep the ciphers for the grain; then just one slip, one idle, incautious act, might have sent him before the magistrates. How could he have convinced them that he was not trying to draw a map but the outline of his former home?

"Do you regret Lacinia?" Mago asked suddenly as if he had guessed his friend's thoughts.

"Of course not," and this was true. He sometimes missed the cold, wild streams tumbling from the hills and the old, easy life at Tarentum but wherever he was, that could never come again. "The Romans destroyed my city, I am thankful to be here." Mago must never know about those ten years at Formiae, friends though they were, nor of the winter that he had spent near Tibur.

"After you went to see the Roman prisoners the other day, I wondered?"

"I only took the peddler's place to oblige him. It was a wasted journey, they hadn't an obol between them and most of them were sick." Yet now that Mago made him think about the camp, he realized that his present intense anxiety dated from that day and the sight of the wasted, hopeless faces of the captives. Was that going to be his own fate? "You were away at a farm or I would have asked your advice. It seemed to me suspicious to refuse, as if in some way I sympathized with them."

"Yes," Mago nodded gravely, "it was a hard point to decide."

"I wonder the magistrates keep them."

"There was some idea that they might be exchanged for Carthaginians taken in Spain but now . . ." he shrugged his shoulders.

"Mago!"

"Yes, Dasius," the captain looked up sharply as if he recognized the urgency in the voice that the trader was trying too hard to keep easy and natural.

"If there is a warning, if you are called back to your ship, can you find a place for me? I am a good swordsman."

"If I go to Carthage it will not be to put to sea. No, stay here where people know you and look after my vines."

"You mean the Carthaginians would not trust me?" He had to know, this was the real fear beneath the apparent anxiety about a landing.

"Be reasonable. You are a stranger and at a time of crisis, some ignorant watchman might shout out 'Roman spy.' Here our neighbors know you are a fugitive from Tarentum and will help you."

Tarentum? He had never seen the place since he had been nine years old and yet it seemed to be the motive force in his life. He had never been so proud as when he had shown that sailor the way to his father's house and had listened to the story of the "golden sands." Yes, ever since he could remember he had wanted to come to Africa but Africa, it appeared, did not want him. "I have never been so happy in my life as here."

"And we shall be happy again even if there are changes. Why should the Romans invade us? They have seized Spain and they are going to have just as much trouble with those savage Iberians as we had. Wait till the harvest is over. Then if I get a good price for my grapes, we will make the trip inland I have promised you so often. Do you know what our real trouble is?"

"No."

"You are a trader and I am a captain, we're both restless."

It was cooler now and almost dark but Mago's habits were as rigid as his principles, he never stirred till he saw the first star in the sky. Then Mago stood up before the statue of the goddess in the courtyard to say the evening prayers. It took a long time because Mago spoke slowly and, although he was not a priest, he began the supplication again if he accidentally missed a word. It was a ceremony that had been handed down from father to son for countless generations and Dasius always stood reverently behind him. It was wise to pray to the powers of the land but although he had seldom gone to the temple, he missed the festivals at Tarentum. There had been less division there between the priests and the worshipers, and the children had carried flowers and cakes up to the altar.

Afterwards they strolled to the shore. "I can't sleep," Mago always joked, "until I have smelt the sea." They seldom spoke as they walked up and down but nothing escaped the captain's observation. He was as Punic as the cone of his cap or a block of his own house. It was different for Dasius, his nerves felt like a cloud of midges tearing at his skin, his heavy robe caught against the middle of his legs, he wanted to do something, anything, rather than wait. Sometimes he wondered if he should try to reach Egypt? A few fishing vessels crept along the coast, transferring the cargoes from one boat to another at some tiny port, so that they were seldom out of sight of land. Yet it was a hazardous voyage and he did not want to leave his friend. There was little to do at the moment and nothing to sell, if only he could work till he was too tired to feel or move, or even talk? They stopped, Mago's eyes swept from point to point of the horizon, it was the signal that their walk was over. "There is no need to fear, Dasius," he said gently, "I will protect you . . . what's that?" He swung round as if the steersman had shifted course too far and pointed. A flame sprang up on the watch tower on the furthest spot that they could see. It was the signal that raiders had been sighted.

What was that scent? The clusters of some African shrub covered the corner of the courtyard and pricked his nostrils as Dasius strode up and down. He did not know or had forgotten its name. Why did people think that he was not a Carthaginian? The breaking of the daily routine had unsettled him as much as it had Mago. He felt it more at the moment than the news that had reached them of the Roman landing. There were no details yet, some of the men had rushed back from the fields because they had seen the beacon on the watch tower but otherwise everything was quiet and, apart from Mago's absence, it was an ordinary, sultry evening.

The captain had gone to Carthage that morning. "It's my duty to report," he had said, rousing Dasius an hour before dawn, "they may need some extra sailors on the warships." No man liked to watch his skills rusting because he had no opportunity to use them and Mago had walked to the gate, the trader had noticed, with a resilience in his movements that had been lacking during the previous months. "I shall be back in a couple of days or if they want me to remain, I will send a messenger to you with my news. Till then, stay inside the house. If people are frightened, they are sometimes hostile to strangers because of their anxiety. Here you are perfectly safe. I do not think myself it is more than a raid. A couple of galleys have landed, burnt a village and taken some prisoners. It cannot be anything serious. Now the magistrates may order out the galleys and if so, we shall soon be able to put to sea ourselves." How happy Mago had looked, the trader thought, how happy!

It had been the captain's chance to return to life but what about himself? The last two years had been "the rest round a well" as the Numidian proverb said but it had been the existence of men whose work was behind them, sitting, talking, doing a little in the fields, going as far as Carthage once a year. It might be a reckless commander, landing, burning and dashing away before he could be caught but brief though the raid might be, it could affect the trader's own life. He had hoped to make a voyage with Mago or if not, to settle in Carthage where there were more opportunities to trade. "Wait," Mago had said, "once you have lived here for three years we can talk to one of the magistrates, that is, if you want to leave me." He knew that his nationality would always be against him. He might tell every stranger that he was a refugee from Tarentum but half the masses did not know where that city was and they distrusted Hannibal, as much, it seemed, as Rome.

He walked up to the shrub and thrust his nose against a flower until the scent stupefied him. It smelt green, he fancied, green as the slopes of a mountain and because he thought of them, he wondered suddenly what had happened to that old rogue, Zonas? He was still breeding donkeys, no doubt, and stuffing himself with kid when he could get it. He had never known a man have such an appetite. Zonas asked for little and had got it whereas he wanted much. He was lonely without Mago and now, he admitted savagely to himself, he was sometimes lonely with him. How could he divest himself not only from the broad aspects of thought but from the trifling gestures and habits to which he had been used since infancy? The long unbelted robes still seemed unfamiliar and the stretches of sitting silently on a bench irksome. He wanted to jump up, run, tie a vine tendril, fetch this or that and sit down again all in the space of an hour. Was it this restlessness that made the Carthaginians dislike him? Yet it made him think the more quickly. Oh, if he had happened to be born in this village, he would now be on the road with Mago, bound for the market place and some possibility of action.

He was quite alone except for an elderly slave. Mago had taken his servant with him and it was the time when the other men were working on the vines. "Stay inside the house . . . stay inside the house . . ." the order rang in ever less listening ears. He walked up and down like the chained lions in front of the temples and wondered if it were true that the priests used a secret method to train these ceremonial beasts? Try as he would now, his former life came back to him, his senses were alert, ready for a bargain or for danger. "Why don't you join us?" an officer had said in Lacinia after watching him at sword practice one morning. He would have agreed, it would have delighted him to have no other care but his weapons and his pay but he had shaken his head, schemed, traded and saved all he could because of a foolish dream that he would never be content till he had landed in Africa.

The scent of the flowers was mingling now with a heap of freshly cut grass. The man at the tavern by the shore had spoken to him about a Numidian girl whom he had recently bought. Perhaps he might look at her? He did not like the ordinary women in the ports and he had never had enough to buy the kind of slave he wanted but what would be the use of silver if the village were looted? "Stay inside the house . . ." but he could not walk up and down all night listening to his inner apprehensions. He went to his room, took a small purse out of its hiding place inside the lining of his cloak and hurried into the kitchen, "you may go to bed when you like," he said to the slave, "I am going to drink a glass of wine with some friends and will fasten the door when I come back. I shall not be late."

The tavern was only half full; most of the villagers had drunk a single cup of wine and had gone home to reassure their families. Dasius sat down on a terrace facing the sea, next to the lattice at the end that kept away the wind. "Has Captain Mago gone to Carthage?" the innkeeper asked, wiping the table with a cloth."

"Yes, he left this morning to ask for orders."

"They'll need him now, he is one of the finest sailors we have."

"Is there any more news?"

"All we know is that two raiders landed and sacked a village. They'll get away before the warships are launched."

Something in the man's voice made Dasius suspect that he was not speaking the truth but being a foreigner and prudent, he made no comment. "I think the captain will be back in a few days."

"I believe it's just a rumor the magistrates have spread before they announce new taxes." The sandalmaker at the next table banged the wood with his fist, he was already a little drunk.

"I am more afraid that they will quarter soldiers here and we shall have to feed them."

"How do we know that they didn't light the fire by accident?"

The continual flow of "I don't believe" or "it isn't possible" irritated Dasius until he wished he had followed Mago's advice and stayed at home. Had his ears caught a man whispering, "careful, that Greek foreigner is here" or was it imagination? He wished he had not let himself sleep for part of the day. He dared not dull his restlessness now with wine although he realized that it was caused by fear. Fear that he would lose Mago, fear of the future. "You miss your friend," the innkeeper came up to the table again, "you were always together in the evening."

"He said he would send for me if he were kept in Carthage."

"It's a pity that the captain never married again, if he had he would be less eager to leave home."

"His wife died while he was on a voyage and Mago told me that he didn't want another until he had finished with the sea."

"Oh, that will be when he dies. But I have got something for you to make you forget your troubles."

"What is it? A last bottle of Campanian?"

"A Numidian girl such as I have not seen for years and so young."

"Smelling of oil and the color of a leather apron."

"You do not trust me but I trust you. You know the fine if the magistrates hear of it though not all of us can marry and what is a traveler to do?"

"Not tonight." He had disobeyed Mago's orders and as soon as he had finished his wine, he must return to the house.

"Don't let a raider frighten you. It's just some sailors looting a few houses up the coast."

"Probably." Dasius tried to appear at ease as the innkeeper moved reluctantly away to greet some villagers who sat down at the one long table on the other side of a row of shrubs in big earthenware pots. The lack of anything to do while his friend was away troubled the trader more than rumors. Yet it seemed strange that no messenger had reached them if it had been a landing from a single ship. A root was burning on the small brazier inside the courtyard, he began to feel drowsy and was half asleep when an angry snarl startled him.

"It's that Greek, clear the spy out before the captain gets back." Dasius shrank against the wall and tried to listen. He thought that he recognized the voice, it was the owner of the only leather shop in the village who spent his earnings on wine and had already stabbed a man in a drunken fight.

"He's harmless enough, what could he do?"

"Light a fire to guide in the galleys."

"They'll never land here, it's too near Carthage."

"You don't know." Dasius peeped through the lattice in spite of his terror and could just see the outlines of the groups sitting round the tables. He would have to pass them eventually to get to the road. "Stone him, fling him into the water or bring him before the magistrates but if you value your homes, though perhaps you don't . . ." the features wrinkled into a grotesque mask rather than a grin, "get rid of that fellow before he does any more mischief."

"I've nothing against him but Captain Mago shouldn't have left him alone in the house." Dasius clenched his fists, why, the speaker was a man who could not even keep his tally sticks in order, he had once spent hours straightening the idiot's accounts.

"Why was the captain here at all? He ought to have been in the city."

"If he couldn't put to sea, it was natural to look after his farm."

"They say he has a good stock of Campanian wine, how about drinking it up for him?"

There was a sudden silence, most of the men had known Mago since childhood.

"Listen to me," a voice broke in from an opposite table, "I am going to ride to Numidia while there is time."

"Numidia! They'll eat you there once your money is finished."

"The first thing to do is to finish off the Roman prisoners. Half their guards marched to Carthage this morning."

"But they may be useful as hostages.'

"Let's find that Greek and chase him into the sea."

"Peace," the innkeeper spoke angrily and sharply. "Do you want to get us all into trouble? Leave everything alone until Captain Mago comes back with his orders or you may find yourselves drafted to work on the walls."

"The safest thing is to ride to Numidia."

The golden sands, Dasius knew now what those words meant, they meant death. It had been shortly after he had heard them that his mother had died and they had left Tarentum. None of the sacrifices he had made in Africa had helped him in the least. Yet the threats had also released some tension in him, he had never felt more alive. "Come," a voice whispered and he swung round to face the innkeeper. The man motioned him to follow and led him through a kitchen where the charcoal fires were dying down under the cooking pots and an old slave drowsed on a mat in the corner. They hurried through a small yard towards a door. "Do you know when the captain will be back?" The innkeeper drew the bolt back slowly so as not to make a noise.

"Soon, he said, but he did not know."

"You had better hide in the fields for a few days till some responsible official returns here to take charge."

"But the house?"

"They will loot it unless you leave. You have time to sleep for a few hours but make your plans carefully. I can hold them off until they start drinking again this evening but no longer."

"And now," Dasius looked up at the sky, "it is almost day."

"Is there any message I can give Captain Mago?"

"Tell him what happened. Tell him if the gods permit we shall meet again in happier times and that I thank him for his kindness."

"May Fortune be with you," the innkeeper looked up and down the street, "go now, no one is in sight."

It was strange to walk along the familiar path and into the courtyard that had been his home for two years, knowing that because of his presence there, a mob might cut down the olives and smash the carefully sealed wine jars in the cellar. A single man, like a single dog, was a friend. A pack of either tore heedlessly whatever they did not like into pieces. What could he do? There was no chance of his reaching Numidia alive even if he wanted to go there. He could hide in a hut till his food gave out or they burned it over him. Would it be better to go to their favorite stretch of sand and slide into the sea of his own free will before a drunken crowd chased him there with rocks? No, he wanted to live . . . wanted to live . . . and a thought surged rebelliously into his mind. Perhaps Mago, that shrewd sailor, had known more about him than he supposed. He had gone back to the prison camp. He had seen the place from a rise in the ground coming back from an errand one day later than he had expected. It was full noon but a Roman had walked over to the thorn bushes. In spite of himself, he had felt sorry for the man and some days later he had invented an excuse to take him past the place again. The officer was there, fighting against his fate and staring moodily at the sky. It should not be difficult to cut a path through the thorns with a sharp knife now that half the guards had been withdrawn to Carthage. He could tell the man that he had also been a prisoner and together they might reach the Roman lines. Africa did not want him and after all, he thought almost with a grimace, half his own blood was Roman. Whatever the temptation, he must not return to Mago and involve him in his own fate. There were plenty of risks in his plan but there was also a chance of life. It was better than sinking into the slime like an unwanted animal with a stone round its neck.

CHAPTER 15

There was no shade. The dirty, gray sand inside the enclosure was full of porridge grits, fish scales and ragged threads of cotton. A musty smell came out of the open door of a low building to the left of the gate. A dozen men sprawled in front of it; they did not move except to slap a mosquito occasionally or to shuffle nearer the grimy wall. "Orbius," a voice called from the end of the row, "you'll never live to lead your horsemen again with such a dismal face. We shall be rescued sometime."

"Rescued, Festus? Oh, leave me alone. You've been saying that for weeks."

"But I heard the slaves shouting something this morning about a foreign ship."

"A captain may have come over about an exchange."

"The food has never been so bad. Unless Rome hurries, the ransom for a plump Carthaginian will be a basket full of our bones."

"Perhaps there has been a landing?" This was such a preposterous idea that everybody laughed.

"Look!" Festus pointed towards the gate, "there are only two sentinels left."

"If there were a landing, they would kill us long before the army arrived." Orbius tilted his straw hat over his nose, it was stifling but if he could get it in just the one position where there were no holes, it shut out the sand, the sky and best of all, the sight of his companions. He did not believe in any rescue. Festus had been with them only eight months. The idiot still had hope.

"But it might be a Roman ship."

"Quiet," a dozen voices yelled at once. It was almost noon and sleep was forgetfulness, the only treasure that they possessed. They had long since exhausted any subject of interest to them and the most innocent word could start a brawl. Orbius pushed his hat a fraction to the right. It would be better to die than go on living in his present misery. He was thirsty but they had all emptied their water bowls by noon and there was no chance of a drink before sunset. Sometimes, just to torment them, the slaves filled the jars up after it was dark so that a soldier could not see if his neighbor had got more than himself. He closed his eyes, he would try for five whole minutes neither to scratch himself nor think, then he would imagine that he was looking up into a dark sky that even the birds could not touch. It was a long time now since he had been out at night although sometimes at midsummer when the nights were almost hotter than the days, an officer would allow them to sleep in the yard and then they sat up for hours, looking in wonder at the stars. It was almost the only pleasure that he had had during the three years of his captivity.

Carthage had turned him into an African; his legs were so dark that he hardly felt the sun on them but he had learned to cover his head. He scratched an insect bite on his neck and because the sky eluded him, he tried to build up in his mind the valley where he had been taken prisoner. First of all, he counted the rushes, clump by clump as they had stretched in front of him, yellow where they rose out of the water, green along the middle of the stems, new like a spring leaf at the feathery tips. He had learned, and in what bitterness, that he ought to have thrust his spear through every tangle to be sure no slingers were using them for cover. How many ripples had there been when he had thrown a pebble idly into the water, five was it or seven, he was never sure because at that moment a stone had thumped against a shield, another had hissed through the air and then, as now, he had seen the Iberians. The only difference was that when he dreamed about them, he imagined that there was time for himself and two others to escape. One would be Karus but who would be the other? Vibius was the better soldier but Briso came from his own estate. Vibius balanced the heavy spears as if they were reeds, Briso would die if he were a captive away from his own hills. He hesitated, the slingers were crawling towards him with a slow, patient movement that they must have learned from lions. "Run!" He must have screamed aloud because his neighbor kicked him. What was he doing, altering his real memories, trying to shield himself from the knowledge that if they had not dropped their weapons to bathe in that stream, he would not be in prison, playing in thought that he had had a chance to escape.

His companions were silent; they were, or were pretending to be, asleep. Only Festus was sitting up. He was trying to mend his shirt with a bit of unraveled cotton and a thorn. It was a hopeless task because the thorn merely widened the rent and the dirty bit of thread would not hold.

Orbius turned over onto his other side and let his blank mind fill with thoughts of water. There was a basin in his father's garden where he had sailed boats as a child, a hollow leaf for a merchantman and a twig for a pirate's galley. He had once sunk his fleet with a push of the hand lest his tutor surprise him playing like a baby. He had then dipped his head into the fountain as an excuse and it was the coolness that he remembered now, that and the splashes that had run down his face to make black dots on the pavement. He was obsessed by rivers, pools, any fresh and moving water but not by the sea. The ocean was a symbol of his voyage into captivity. "If only they had killed me," he muttered, the sweat was pouring from his body but he could not lie still, he sprang up and walked across the sand although the midday sun was said to bring fevers to those who exposed themselves to it, past Festus who was sucking a pricked finger, past the heap where they threw the broken bits of earthenware, on and on at the back of the hut until he came to the hedge of poisonous thorns that kept the prisoners inside the camp more securely than guards or walls. Occasionally a man went mad and flung himself against the barbs. He always died although Orbius suspected that it was merely for lack of a physician or an antidote and not because the poison itself was deadly. He had

175

scratched himself once gently as an experiment. The wound had festered but it had gradually healed. He walked beside the hedge, trembling with rage, knowing that if Festus spoke to him again that day, he would fly at the boy's throat. Perhaps he would catch a summer fever in this sun and die in this alien, merciless land? No, not like that, not stupidly on a pallet, babbling about water. Not before he had told that fool, Fabius Maximus, what he thought of him. Wait, watch, fight no major battles, and the State rewarded the graybeard with an army while the young men who had served it were left to rot in these filthy, stinking camps. The best years of his manhood were behind him. Was there never to be a recompense for the sufferings that he had neither willed nor deserved? Was nothingness itself not nobler than the degradations of his present life? He had never had patience with men who had sought initiation, not even with his friend Karus. What did priest or Pythagorean know more than a man himself about his end? It was the day he valued, this dual day that had once been full of struggle and laughter and was now as bitter as the dust of this verminous, forgotten camp.

He walked slowly towards a spot almost at the end of the enclosure where the bushes did not grow quite so closely together and where, by lying on the ground, it was possible to see the sand on the free side of the barrier. Two men had made a dash for liberty at that point a few months previously but had stuck midway among the thorns. Their companions had dragged them back, the guards had laughed, but both had died within a couple of days from the poisoned gashes all over their bodies. Orbius started as he came to the place. It had nothing to do with Festus and his wild guesses but several of the bushes seemed to have withered away and when he stooped, several stems seemed to have been sliced through at the level of the ground.

Suppose he pulled his hat over his head and tried to butt his way across what was now almost a gap? He might die but had he any choice otherwise except to return to his place in the line and wait with nothing to break the days except the occasional visit of some trader who sold food and clothes (a slave would have rejected them) at three times their value to a newcomer who still had a coin or two in his possession? The other prisoners, men like himself who had been in the camp for years and had nothing left, got rags to replace their own rags only from the dead.

The thought of water was becoming so intense that he seemed to see it spreading across the sand. All he wanted was to taste and hear it. Sometimes his friends had shouted that a pool was rising in the middle of the camp. They had been happy for a moment but after they had sprung up from their flea ridden mats to look for it in vain, they had often died. He would count ten and dash. One . . . two . . . the words turned into a scream.

"Not that way," a voice whispered in Latin, "it's too dangerous."

Orbius pushed back his hat, too startled to speak. A figure was crouching in the sand, then he recognized the face. It was the man who had replaced their usual trader on the last visit. He remembered him because he had given a prisoner something for his fever without payment. "Who are you?" He wondered for a brief moment if the fellow was trying to provoke him so that he could denounce him to the guard?

"My name is Dasius. I am a citizen of Neapolis. I was taking goods and slaves to a merchant in Sicily when our ship was captured. Like yourself, I want to return to my home. If I help you to escape, will you give me your protection?"

"I will treat you as my kinsman if we get away but where can we find a ship?"

"There is a rumor that a Roman fleet has landed, thirty miles from here."

"An army! A landing! I must tell my comrades at once."

"Wait! It may be a tale. Besides, even if you overpowered the guards here, there are many soldiers camped beyond the village. Most of you could not walk three miles and from what I hear it is merely a raid. Our chance is speed. Come with me and we may yet be able to save your companions."

Orbius looked back. The man was right. Only Festus whose gaiety was so irritating and perhaps two more were in a state to march. "What do you want me to do?" he asked, looking at the hedge. There were still about a dozen stalks to be cut.

"Move to the right. I am going to throw a knife over. I have been working on this gap for hours. I would have come last evening but at night they let out the dogs."

A small object hurtled through the air. It was a freshly sharpened dagger rolled in a piece of felt. "Wrap the stuff round your hand," the voice continued, "and cut as closely to the ground as you can. The thorns are not as deadly as they say but if you get one in a finger, it may fester for weeks."

Orbius slashed violently but the pith was tough and turned the blade. Suppose Festus saw him? He was more afraid of that clumsy youth than of the guard. He was capable of shouting so that the sentinels heard him, "are you trying to escape?" It seemed an hour although it was actually only minutes until it was clear enough for him to see Dasius raking away the bushes that he had cut with a crooked stick. "I am going to throw you a blanket," the trader whispered. "Wrap it round you, keep your head down and run but be sure to bring back the knife."

He hurled himself forward, there was a sharp pain as the spines ripped his leg, a spike struck him cruelly across the shoulders but he pitched forward suddenly onto the open sand. Dasius snatched away the blanket. "Look!" he held it up, "it is full of thorns."

"May Fortune be praised! Have you water? They never gave us enough to drink."

"Not here but I am taking you to a well. It is lucky that you have on sandals."

Orbius nodded. Most of his companions went barefooted but he had exchanged his last spare garment for a pair rather than touch the slimy fish bones round the hut without some protection. He stooped to look at the gashes along his leg.

"Can you run? I doubt if they discover your escape before the evening but the guards can see us here. The sooner we move the better."

"Get me away from this camp."

He followed Dasius towards the track a short distance away full of an exhilaration that he was never to feel again. It was hard to breathe, the blood was running down his leg and shoulder and crazy impulses stirred inside his head, thoughts that he had not allowed himself to think for months, a foolish certainty that whatever happened, he would not be recaptured Yet it was a long time since he had even run across the enclosure and he dropped an ever increasing number of paces behind the trader until they turned a corner, left the camp behind them and saw the village at the edge of a shallow bay. "Oh," he shouted as Dasius waited for him to come up, "a ship, a ship," and he pointed towards a fishing boat in the distance. It floated like a toy on the smooth, blue water and was the first one that he had seen for years.

"It's not far now." Dasius opened a door in a wall surrounding a small house and then shut it carefully behind them. There was a well in the middle of the courtyard and there, in defiance of all the rules that he had learned while training, Orbius plunged his head into a bucket that stood beside it and drank until he could drink no more. It was not the sparkling water of his native mountains, it was flat and stale, but finer than the choicest Campanian wine at such a moment. "Wait here. The house is empty and I am going to get you some clothes, but there are neighbors down the road. Do not speak and above all, do not move from here."

The unaccustomed running and the water that he had drunk so hastily half stupefied Orbius and he sat down on a bench in front of the fountain and tried to get back his breath. He splashed water over his head and down his legs till his wits began to return to him and he could notice the trees standing along one side of the wall. It was a pleasant, peaceful place but unnaturally still. Had his rescuer gone to call the guard so as to get the reward for capturing an escaped prisoner? Ought he to run out to the desert? He would be seized in a moment in his torn clothes. He sprang up but at that moment Dasius hurried out of the house with a bundle under his arm and a saucer of yellow ointment in his hand. He himself had left behind the ragged tunic in which he had been working and was dressed like a farmer with what appeared to be a new Numidian blanket over his shoulder. "It's hot now," he explained as he saw Orbius looking at it, "but it will be cold tonight."

"In Lotus Land there is always water," Orbius said gaily as the trader began to smear the salve a little more thickly than was necessary over his scratches. Dasius nodded, he had never been so unhappy since his boyhood at Formiae. Whatever happened, he would never see Mago again and he had had to leave most of his possessions in his room. Each of them marked a bargain or some incident in his travels. "Get into these clothes as quickly as possible," he said sharply, "we must leave the village before the people wake. I know a farm along the coast where we can shelter for the night."

They were not far from the sea. If there were no other way out, Orbius thought, he would jump into it. Death was better than another captivity. How much longer could he lift his smarting legs? They had walked for hours, losing the way, finding it again, stepping across narrow irrigation runnels, on and on until the sun had set and it was dark. His present exhaustion had dulled the beautiful moment of his escape. Let philosophers preach what they would, a man's mind was at the mercy of the discomforts of his body. "Are you sure we are on the right road?" he asked abruptly. He owed Dasius gratitude, without his help he would still be in that dreadful camp but he was suspicious of the man's motives.

Surely no master would have left his slave alone in the house unless he had believed him to be faithful to Carthage?

"At least we are walking in the right direction." Dasius kept his eyes fixed on the sky. The idle evenings when Mago had tried to show him how a captain guided his ship by the stars, might be the means of saving their lives. He had twice accompanied his friend to a farm further along the coast but they had walked there in the cool hours of the morning and spent most of the day gossiping in a shady courtyard and eating the honey sweetened pulse for which the district was famous. His sack was heavy and he was about to shift it to his other shoulder when he heard a shout as if somebody were calling a dog. "Lie down," he whispered, dragging his companion into a shallow ditch a little distance from the road, "in spite of your clothes, they may recognize you as Roman."

It was too dark to see the faces distinctly but Dasius was sure that it was the farmer and his family. They were driving an ox and a small donkey in front of them. Women followed with baskets on their heads, one of which, to judge from the squawks, was full of fowls. Other farmers must have joined them because there were boys driving a flock of sheep and Mago's friend owned olive trees but no pasture. He strained his ears to hear what they were saying but was too far away to catch more than an occasional angry command to the animals. He dug his fingers into the earth in his impatience, letting it slip in its richness through his fingers. Every handful represented the toil of generations. This plain rather than the city, was the heart of the empire and if some mounted troops destroyed the irrigation channels it would be worse than burning down the port; there would be no more olives and no more corn. If Rome won, his hand slipped instinctively towards his dagger, these peasants who had the feeling of their land in their blood would end their days as porters or crawling along mine shafts while the fields reverted to the poisonous thorns that he had cut away that morning and that the Carthaginians had driven back, step by step, from the rim of the coast to the ridged sands of Numidia.

Dasius waited until the last straggler passed, then he shook Orbius who had fallen asleep. "We cannot be far now from the farm, there is a well in the courtyard and we can rest there till it is light." It was easy to follow the hoof prints in the by now well trampled path but he was preoccupied by the course to be taken next day and did not see a bundle until he kicked it and it whimpered. A child began to howl, it must have been left behind. He picked it up and put it on his shoulder, it was, he judged, about three years old.

"You are not going to take a child with us!" The Roman's voice was full of horror.

"No, but it will be an excuse to ask those people for their news. Here, take my pack for me, and wait."

"While you denounce me to the Carthaginians."

"Should I have risked my life cutting those thorns almost in sight of the guards unless I had wanted to help you escape?"

"Forgive me," yet try as he would, Orbius mistrusted the trader, "I have been away from my countrymen so long, I am suspicious even of a twig."

"They may know where the ships have actually landed. Stay here, I shall soon be back."

It took him longer than he expected, however, to

catch up with the party. The infant was heavy and he was very tired. He realized that he had awakened the Roman's suspicions but how could he leave the son of one of Mago's friends to wander off alone into the bushes and die there from hunger or snake bite? Even now his heart drew him back to the city that he loved but "that Greek is a spy" still rang in his ears and he must remember Mago's safety. "Wait!" he yelled as soon as he got within hailing distance, "wait, you've lost one of the children."

A shepherd heard him first. They stopped but let him walk all the way up to them with slow, weary steps. "It's my grandchild," an old woman shrieked, "you swore the child was on the donkey."

"He must have slipped off when we halted," a man said, coming forward anxiously and holding out his arms to the child. The boy began to cry and then, recognizing his father, stopped whimpering and laughed.

"Come with us, the Romans are behind us, slaying as they go."

"Far behind?"

"If it were light you could see their dust."

"No, not that near," a herdsman pushed a ewe that kept turning in the wrong direction back into line, "but they'll be here by dawn."

"They took taxes from us to hire men for the army," the farmer luckily had not recognized Dasius in the darkness, "and now, where are the soldiers? Who is going to pay me for my farm?"

"They may not have time to burn down the house."

"They will."

"Get the flocks moving, why are we lingering here? You brought the child, you can join us if you like."

"I came with another man to fetch my master's horse

and he is holding it for me. I will fetch him and join you at the next halt." Two sheep dashed by, followed by a dog. They knocked a basket over that a woman was resting against a stone and the trader took advantage of the confusion to walk and eventually run to where Orbius was waiting for him. "The Romans are nearer than I thought," he panted, "if we hide in one of the outhouses of the farm till day comes, they will find us themselves and we may get a ride back to their camp." Unless, he reflected ironically, both got arrows through them before Orbius could identify himself to their commander.

They were rescued the next morning in broad daylight if rescue were the proper word to apply, as Dasius wondered, to the chance arrival of a troop of scouts. They were wakened from a sound sleep by hooves clattering up to the courtyard and a young Roman, instinctively brushing away the dust from his shield as he reined up his horse, stared in surprise as they emerged from their hiding place. "I am a Roman officer," Orbius said, stepping forward and saluting, "I have been a prisoner in a camp nearby for three years."

"A prisoner?" The man seemed unimpressed, "where are the Carthaginians?"

"They were falling back on the city."

"And who is this man?" The officer pointed at Dasius.

"A trader from Formiae who was taken captive at sea. He helped me to escape."

"The coast seems deserted except for a few peasants. Surely they have troops somewhere covering their withdrawal?" He was young and eager for a fight.

"We saw none yesterday but can you free my companions? There are about sixty of us in the camp, most of them sick and unable to walk."

"It depends on the distance.'

"With your horses, about three hours."

"Too far. My orders are not to ride further than two hours away from the army. Besides, what could we do with sixty men if they are sick? Two of my soldiers will take you up behind them and you can make a full report at our headquarters. Where did you say you were taken prisoner?"

"It was in a skirmish three days south of Rome." Orbius stared round him in humiliation, he saw that the officer only half believed his story and his legs were so painful that he had to be lifted onto the horse. "They haven't wasted much food on you," one of the men said compassionately, noticing the wasted limbs. Dasius also pretended to mount with difficulty lest they doubt his story of having been a slave. He glanced round the courtyard that had been so full of activity and friendliness the previous autumn. What had the farmer once said over their meal? "Let them withdraw the Commander and his army. If we stay in Africa and leave the Romans alone, we have nothing to fear." To Mago's relief, he had not argued with the man. How could he have explained the struggle between empires to an olive grower who had never left his trees during his life?

A soldier leaned forward and slashed the vine growing round one of the pillars for no other reason than to test the sharpness of his dagger. Another kicked a hole through the water jug by the door. Let them think the tears in his eyes came from joy at his rescue, Dasius thought savagely and then the same urge to live that had sent the farmer and his family stumbling towards Carthage through the darkness made him mutter aloud so that the soldiers could hear him, "praise be to Fortune

for my rescue, I will sacrifice a chicken at the first temple
I reach."

"Why are those men lingering in the hold?" Orbius
shouted. He clenched his fists in frustration, he was lonely
and even this light work tired him. They had offered
him a place on a ship but how could he return to the
home that was leagues away across that open sea until
he had led his horsemen against the enemy? A thorn in
his leg that had been overlooked had kept him inside a
shelter for a week, dreaming of water and wondering if
he had escaped only to die? He still could not ride. Nobody had time to spare for a former prisoner. The dedi-
cation of the officers when it had hardly seemed possible
that Rome could survive had now changed into a ribald
indifference in the army towards anything but comfort.
Destiny! Whoever had said that a man should accept
good and evil as it came to him? He should be the master of circumstances, never their victim. He still repeated
to himself that it would have been better if the slingers
had killed him outright; at least he would have been
buried in his native land and spared these humiliations.
He was free, yes, he swung round to look at the scene
behind him, hundreds of men marching up the beach
with heavy jars on their shoulders or their heads and as
many coming down empty handed in a second line towards the ships. There was activity everywhere but here
he was, trying not to put too much weight on his band-
aged leg, checking stores instead of galloping forward
with the horsemen.

Dasius smoothed the wax on yet another tablet. His
African adventure had ended; a trader had no opportunities in a plundered country but he had done several

small services for a captain aboard one of the galleys
and he was sure of a passage soon to Neapolis. Meantime he was earning a few obols a day. "Why do they
send us all these cooking pots?" he grumbled, "there's
a potter in every village." A mound of broken earthenware had already accumulated at one end of the camp.
A guard had seen several vipers crawling out of it and
he and his companions had smashed the sherds to bits
with their heavy sticks. "What we need are more sandals.
These sands burn a man's feet unless he is African born."

"And reins! Whatever have they done with the reins?
Trebius told me this morning that he had had to leave
two men in camp because of broken bridles."

Dasius dropped his stylus and stooped to pick it up.
The angry Roman must not notice that he was smiling
but the words reminded him of a dirty, frightened figure
with a cracked head coming towards him down a village
street. He wondered what had happened to Zonas? He
missed the broad face and the shrewd bits of observation
more than he had expected. It always surprised him
how apparently haphazard incidents fitted into one another. If it had not been for that chance meeting he
would still be taking his earnings back to Alfius, he
would never have seen Carthage and missed what he
knew to have been the happiest years of his life.

A group of slaves toiled down the gangplank laden
with sacks. "Open a load," Dasius commanded as the
first ones reached the quay. Orbius turned sharply, his
thoughts had been elsewhere and he reflected that the
Greek was being a much better officer at that moment
than himself. An overseer ripped away the top covering
and laughed.

"What is it? Take something out. Find out what's inside."

"Cooking pots!" Even the slaves laughed.

Orbius was the only man who did not smile. He felt his body burning not with heat but rage. Such a mistake could send men into a prison camp to rot and die. He stooped, picked up a pot and hurled it into the sea. "Here," he said to Dasius, "take these tally sticks to the store and tell them what has happened. The trumpet will sound in a moment and it's not worth unloading more of that rubbish tonight."

It was almost sunset and Orbius struggled a few steps further until he had passed the ship and was nearly at the end of the quay. The water was too smooth to count the waves and brought the terrible isolation of the sand back to his mind. It had haunted all prisoners at one moment or another. The three best years, the great years of a man's life had been taken from him and he would know no peace until he had ridden against the Numidians. They had brought his companions to the camp while he was lying ill and they had gone gratefully home on the first galley. None of them had suggested staying with the army. He could accept defeat in a freely chosen contest but the stupidity of his imprisonment hurt him more than the poison that had almost cost him his life. He turned and hobbled towards the beach again where the slaves were trying to wash off the dust of the day in a scum of water that was full of broken pots.

"Trebius sent me to ask if the bridles have arrived."

There was something familiar about the voice but the officer was not wearing armor and Orbius did not know to which troop he belonged. "We are two horsemen short until we can get the reins," the voice continued patiently, then he recognized the unmistakable tilt of the head. "Karus," he yelled, "Karus!" and grasped him by both shoulders.

The officer stared. The face in front of him was that of an old man with a tooth missing from the front of the mouth but there was no mistaking the smile. "Orbius! It can't be, yes, it is, oh, Orbius, how did you get to Africa? I've been trying to ransom you for years."

"They sent us to Carthage and paraded us through the streets and then they shut us up in a camp. I almost died there. We heard about the landing and I escaped the same day."

The evening trumpet sounded. They looked at each other, somehow ill at ease. "I've changed, I know," Orbius stammered, "my leg was poisoned and I'm checking stores till I can ride. No, there are no bridles for you. Guess what the fools have sent? A cargo of cooking pots all the way from Ostia." It broke the strangeness and they both laughed. "And I had merchants looking for you all over Lacania," Karus said, "but nobody could find you. Come to my tent at once and tell me all that happened."

CHAPTER 16

"If my friend Orbius needs a guide, would you take him
to Neapolis? He does not know that short cut through
the mountains and it would give you the chance that
you have always wanted to go and see your friends at
Formiae on your way back."

Zonas lifted his hat and scratched his head. He almost wished that Karus had never asked him the question. Even if it were a calm day the wind was always
hiding somewhere and it was the same with a man's
birthplace. He forgot it for months at a time, then the
sudden smell of a wet strap drying in the sun brought
some unimportant incident back to him or a fisherman
shouting (it was always the same old man with a white
circle on his brown sail) "a fresh sole, Zonas, just out of

the net, a sole for a cup of wine," and Formiae would be round him again so vividly that he began stepping over acorns as if they were cobbles.

He wanted to go, he wanted to stay. Ten years was a long time and, in spite of what people said, the seasons were never quite the same. The third year had been the time of the drought when, in spite of his care, many animals had died. The fifth summer there had been double the usual quantity of wine and they had had to make a special journey to Tibur to get more jars for it. Karus had returned to the villa after the battle in Africa but he spent the winters in Rome. All the same, he was more interested in the farms than anyone had expected and had even bought an additional vineyard and some pasture.

What were those sheep doing so far down the hill? Zonas sprang up from the old tree trunk on which he was sitting and began to pace restlessly up and down. His eyes fell on three white daisies and a fern growing out of a rut where a wheel had once slipped from the path, he could feel the pull towards his birthplace, "a city replaces a man's parents once they are dead," but it rubbed like a piece of grit against the fear that Fortune might protect him no longer if he left this valley. Where was Melania? She always brought the first meal up to him at this particular spot and it flattered him that she carried it up herself instead of sending the mule boy although she insisted strictly otherwise upon her freedwoman status. She was not late but he wanted to talk to her.

Melania had noticed him coming down earlier than usual from the upper pasture and was hurrying up the path. It was fortunate, she thought, plucking and tasting a stalk, that she had herded goats throughout her childhood. She knew the different grasses in each field and where the plants grew that poisoned the ewes. What a pity that just today she would have to tell him about the beans! They were turning black and he would be angry just as she wanted him to find a stone to replace the worn step in front of the kitchen.

How times had changed! Looking back, she could just see the red tiled roof of the house in the slaves' quarter where she had been born. Who would have imagined then that she would ever be free? Zonas need not think that he was the only one to feel the call of spring; when Domina Sybilla had taken her away from the herds to put her into the spinning room, she had run away. A charcoal burner had taken her back to the villa and, to her surprise, her mistress had not beaten her. "I should like to be up in the meadows myself but we have our duties here." Domina Sybilla had let her work a little in the garden or sometimes help the cook until the worst of her wildness had subsided. All her present happiness was due to her mistress and she never neglected to lay a wreath on the tomb on the proper day or to think of her whenever she went down to the villa.

"You are late," Zonas said, sitting down on the tree trunk once more and lifting the cloth from the basket.

"After you have eaten, Zonas," it was better to tell him the bad news at once, "I want you to look at the beans. Half the plants in the first row are black."

"There is always something," his tone was milder than she had expected, "first we had the war and the army took the men, then we could get no material for the tools and now the crops go wrong. Last year it was the barley, this year it's the beans. Mocco told me that the farmer by the river has lost his whole crop but he always sows them too soon."

"At least the war is over," Melania accepted gratefully the piece of bread that Zonas offered her, although she had already eaten in the kitchen, it was a good sign when he wanted to share his meal. "I was always afraid that you would leave with some levy."

"Oh, I should have taken to the hills."

"And what would have happened to the farm and your sons?" Men might be better at carrying timber but they had no sense.

"Karus asked me last night if I would take his friend to Neapolis."

"Are you going with him?" Somehow she was not afraid, there were no Numidians now in the hills and with the Roman's armed servants as escort, the roads would be safe.

"He's a surly fellow. He grumbled about my giving Sikelia her oats after I had paid for them myself."

"I doubt that the master likes him as much as he pretends." She had noticed Karus taking his usual solitary walk every evening. "And they have only been here two days."

"The man was a prisoner for several years. You can grow away from people as you can from animals. If you sell a mule, it won't recognize you if you see it again at some market."

"Are you going with him?" Melania asked a second time. She would have to prepare some food and she hoped that he might have enough time to change the kitchen step for her.

Zonas looked across to the great shoulder of the mountain, it was glowing in the heat like the flank of a horse.

Orbius would spare neither his men nor himself. He would go back to Formiae but was this the moment? The mare was due to foal before he could get back and now there was this trouble with the beans. He took another slice of bread out of the basket and heard himself answering to his own surprise, "only if it is the master's orders. We are late with the work this spring."

"At least Neapolis is not as far as Sicily but it seems a pity you have to leave so soon."

"It is only for a year, Karus." Orbius stretched his arms above his head as if he, like the lizards, were awakening from a winter sleep. "I should have preferred to go back to the army."

Karus looked down a long line of almost obliterated steps that had once led down to the plain. The farmers everywhere had begun to repair the paths but supplies were still scarce and it often took years. He knew that his friend was angry because after two severe illnesses he had been sent back to Italy and given a post in the south but most officers would have considered themselves lucky. Men were ready to serve their city in a time of danger but a camp after the war was a barren place.

"Neapolis was loyal." Orbius yawned and kicked a pebble down the hill, listening as it bumped and rolled to a standstill in the distance. "I should not complain if it were a different mission but they are sending me there because I once spoke Carthaginian. I've spent eight years trying to forget those barbarous sounds."

"But what is the use of Carthaginian in Neapolis?"

"Sailors come there from many different ports. There is trouble again at Carthage and some of these men may bring us news. We should never have left Africa until we had burnt that city to the ground. Hannibal is trying to make himself dictator."

"They have no fleet. As long as they pay us the tribute does it matter?"

"None of you will believe in the danger." Orbius slapped the stone balustrade in irritation. "I have been their prisoner and I know." Almost every week he dreamed about that stinking, greasy camp and woke up wishing that he had died. "Our youth is corrupt. They think of their own pleasure and forget the gods."

"And laugh too much." Karus expected his friend to smile because if he could find the right word, there was still a sudden flash of sympathy between them but Orbius sat as stiffly as if on parade. "We must not relax our vigilance for a moment. I wish you would take my warning seriously."

"I do, but why should we deprive the young of their moment of gaiety? They grew up in privation."

"I had hoped to command my legion. My illness was the direct result of my imprisonment."

"But we want to make you forget it." Karus tried to keep the exasperation out of his voice. There was a piece of warm yellow brick lying among the white pebbles, the bees were beginning to hum among the flowers beyond the ilex, "oh, love something even if it is only a lizard," he wanted to say because he had heard in Rome that Orbius had been recalled less on account of his fever than because he had quarreled with his fellow officers but there would be no response. His friend would never leave the prison bars behind him till he died.

Orbius sprang up and walked the length of the terrace. His nerves were like thorns if he had to sit still any length of time. He could not question his companion's loyalty because Karus had fought to the end of the African campaign but he also knew that he moved in circles in Rome that were fascinated by the empire they had defeated. They even discussed if there were priesthoods south of Numidia older than the ones in Greece and, if so, what were the doctrines? All a man needed was courage and the help of Fortune but he had missed this last gift. "I've heard," he said, "that the trader who helped me escape has settled near Neapolis. If so, and I can find him, he might be useful."

"He will not like Carthage any more than you do."

"No, but he spoke the language and I suppose he has friends among the sailors who come to the town." Somehow, in spite of the gratitude that he knew he owed to Dasius, he was mistrustful of the man; why had he been free to come and go as he liked unless the Carthaginians believed him loyal to them?

"Their trade is finished. Besides, Hannibal is an old man. He could never raise another army."

"He wants to break the power of the suffetes and to do this, he is flattering the people and promising them honesty in the markets. If he gained control, he might win back the Numidians."

"Not in our lifetime. No, Orbius, go to Baiae and get them to wash this fever out of your blood."

"Perhaps, when I have finished my work." No draughts of water, no words, could obliterate the interview that he had had with the commander in Rome. "We all know that you have suffered," the man had said almost angrily, "but to let it color every deed and word when the war has been over so many years, is a form of defeat." Life had ended for him at that moment. He could only do his duty and hope that one day they might remember he had warned them. "I must leave tomorrow," he would be more at ease on the road than trying to revive a friendship that he had almost forgotten, "can my horses be ready the third hour after sunrise?"

"So soon?" Karus noticed, almost with horror, that he could not suppress a feeling of relief that he could return the next day to his ordinary life without having to watch his tongue constantly in case some chance word reminded Orbius of the years that he had lost, "would you like Zonas to guide you through the passes?"

"No, I am anxious to get to my post as soon as possible and I have decided to follow the main road."

He had failed his friend in some way but could even a priest break through such a barrier of mistrust? Then Karus was angry that such a thought had come into his mind and said with an unnecessary warmth, "I shall ride with you to the end of the valley and if you go to Baiae in the summer, send me a messenger, and I will join you there to drink the waters myself."

The terrace looked directly down to the sea. A warship was rowing slowly into the harbor, the bright red sails of many scattered boats raced towards the port and as Dasius watched, a knot of people, they were only black dots from this height, separated and came together again as soon as they saw where the fishermen would land their catch. The hillside was cool; the distance kept unwanted visitors away although he was not living in any dangerous isolation. There were a dozen houses around him, each occupied by men like himself who wanted to enjoy a few quiet years before they died, away from the noise and tumult of Neapolis.

The garden was almost bare. He had purposely kept it free from many plants. There was a fountain because he liked water, a few roses, each from some special place, and a fig tree to remind him of Africa. He owned the kitchen garden behind the house and a small vineyard. If he had any complaints, his eyes wandered from bay to island and from shore to hill, it was that there were too many cities in sight. He had been a trader, he knew that markets were necessary but he preferred now to look at grass rather than at red tiled roofs.

It was the moment of the day that he liked most, he had a friend beside him, and he was free to enjoy it. "I am glad you have come, Kallistus," he glanced at the Greek who was sitting beside him on the bench, "I am becoming a barbarian. Do you know it is a full month since I invited any of my neighbors to dinner?" They had not had to sit in smoky inns as he had, being polite to villagers in the hope of selling them his master's wares.

"You have had more experiences than most of us to fill your mind." Kallistus jerked at his cloak, it had caught on an angle of the wall, and he smoothed a wrinkle out in the white linen. "You were either dreaming or asleep when I arrived."

"I was thinking about Zonas, that peddler I once knew." He wondered if he would still recognize the round face under the dirty, straw brimmed hat if they happened to meet? The man had actually enjoyed the airless, dirty hovels and the ever repeated arguments about the best way to treat a mule's galled back. Yet if that ragged, disreputable fellow had not recognized a belt buckle, he himself would never have found the Carthaginian camp. Life itself was a series of steps, they were uneven and did not always follow a straight line, but again it was only because he had learnt some Punic at the summer camp in the hills that they had sent him off to Tibur to gather news and given him a post in Lacinia afterwards. He had met the merchant who had warned him to leave over a deal in leather and oil. Whatever happened, he had seen the "Mistress of the Seas." He had had his two years with Mago and through his half unwilling escape he had returned to Italy with enough stores to sell in the period of scarcity after the war so that he was able to live, very simply it was true, on his own ground with a single slave and a boy to help with the vines, looking less at the stars than at the ever changing motion of the sea, spread like some great turquoise at his feet, and at the ships that now spring had come sailed out of the harbor.

"Are you sure it was the peddler and not Tarentum? You have the Greek perception and a Roman's energy. If your father had given you a sword instead of a stylus, you would have forgiven him for uprooting you from your birthplace."

"Never!" Kallistus might understand the interplay of numbers that moved like the waves from some invisible center to dissolve and flow again in an ever revolving disk but it was speculation. He had never followed a captain down a shady street while the man told him of the long necked birds kept to peck grains of gold out of the sand on the far side of Numidia. It was not imagination. He had seen donkeys in Carthage laden with baskets of their eggs. They were sometimes used for the funeral ceremonies.

"Our Neapolis was meant for you," Kallistus continued, "Greek, Iberian, Roman, all beginnings are reconciled here, it's not a city, it's a world."

"I have never seen a Carthaginian sailor."

"Use your eyes," his friend looked at him mockingly. "Poor wretches, they were bred to the sea and what else can they do? If they spoke of their birthplace, they would not be allowed to land but they slip in occasionally on the Egyptian galleys."

"Good or bad, we are all the slaves of life but I feel sometimes that the scales are overloaded."

"Come to us, Dasius, Fortune has given you peace after your wanderings. All our feelings are transient, they are the reflection of something that we cannot understand before Hermes summons us or, as our master Pythagoras has said, until we are ready to live again."

"One life is enough." The flaw might be small but nothing reached perfection in either landscape or friend. Even at this moment when he was ready to give his full attention to his visitor's words, Dasius knew that Kallistus had never been exposed to the brutal realities of the road. "If a fly stings your neck when you are selling oil, the irritation is so distracting that I have sometimes lost a handful of obols in order to scratch the bite instead of making a bargain."

"You could withdraw into yourself as they teach in the temples of healing."

Dasius looked up angrily only to find that his friend was laughing at him. "You are wasting your time. I should like to know the cause behind a man's actions but I have been through too many dangers to listen to theories. What map can any man know thoroughly but his own?"

"There were even some of us at Carthage. A trader who escaped shortly before the Roman landing told us about them. They were all Greeks."

"I heard of some carpenters who worshiped in a temple of their own. The laws were strict everywhere in the city except in the district round the harbor. So many foreigners lived there that they let us alone."

"It is many years now since we had news from them. Perhaps they have forgotten our teaching. We should have liked to help them but it was impossible."

"There was no need to destroy the smaller ships. The Romans would have had the tolls if they had permitted some trade."

"I grew up wondering which side would be the victor. Perhaps it was this uncertainty, the need to protect myself from a continual fear that Neapolis might be sacked, that turned me towards what you call my useless studies?"

"Carthage was old. The barbarians are young and always win. They follow their impulses and do not reason."

The sun caught the rim of the amphora by the fountain and divided it into two sharp patterns of light and dark red. "I am happy here," Dasius brushed away a leaf that had fallen on the seat beside him, "I like you to talk even if I do not agree with you." It was the real reward, reserved perhaps for age, to have a friend whose mind soared with one's own. Mago had been nearer to him but with always a feeling of reserve on the captain's part, due to the stiffness of the Punic training. What had happened to him? Had he had to watch his ship being burnt? "All we are given is the moment, everything else we lose."

They were so absorbed in watching the sky begin to darken at the edge of the bay that neither of them noticed the footsteps coming up the path and it was only when Dasius heard a voice say harshly, "I know your master" that he jumped to his feet. An official in a toga stood in front of him. He glanced apprehensively at the figure and recognized Orbius.

"It's been so long since we parted on the wharf at Utica," Dasius said after the customary greetings were over, "that if I had met you in a crowded street, I might not have recognized you."

"I had a poisoned leg and three years of prison food behind me when you saw me last."

"It is an honor to welcome you to my house." Kallistus bowed and slipped away, an anxious look on his face. Dasius sent his servant for wine and stood, as was fitting in front of the Roman who had taken his seat on the bench. Orbius motioned him to sit down beside him and the trader obeyed uneasily; why, oh why, had he tempted Fortune by telling his friend that he was happy?

"I think your Africans must have cursed me. I nearly died from fever in Sicily last summer. Eventually they sent me back to Rome." The words tasted like a rotten olive, Orbius thought, every time that he had to use them.

"So you have come to the springs at Baiae!" Dasius could hardly restrain his relief. "I know a man who went there with a stick and came back able to run."

"Oh, I may go there for a few days in the spring but I am here on a different errand."

The trader's anxiety returned but he tried not to show it in his face.

"I had hoped to have commanded a legion before I died but that cannot be, thanks to those Africans. I told them in Rome I was too young to retire to my estate and so they have sent me to gather news about Carthage."

"Carthage! But the city is ruined. What can they do?"

"Rome is in danger as long as Hannibal lives and last year he was elected magistrate."

"There has been talk in the market place but I did not listen to it," without knowing why, Dasius scratched his ear. "Like yourself, I wanted to forget the years I spent there."

"You were in a merchant's house and clothed and fed."

"I was not free."

Orbius looked down at the pattern of white and red stones under his feet. The place was austere, it could have belonged to a Roman, there was something about Dasius that made him different from an ordinary merchant and yet he hated the man. "That is why I have come to see you. We believe that Hannibal is trying to overthrow the government and impose great changes upon Carthage."

"Would it matter to Rome? They have no fleet and can get no mercenaries." The Iberian slingers joined the legions and the Gauls stayed at home.

"Hannibal is trying to dispossess the men who signed the treaty with us. It is merely a wasp's nest if you like but we do not want another war. I see that you do not agree with me."

"Oh, but I do," Dasius answered hurriedly, "I was puzzled because I thought it was Hannibal who had insisted upon making peace."

"Leave the politics to us," Orbius said sharply. "We have people there watching our interests but I promised to send a messenger to them this spring. I thought of you because I need a man who speaks Punic and whom I can trust. You will sail on a merchantman to Carthage next week. You have only to see my friends, pick up any news you can and return on the same boat to Neapolis."

"I am getting old. I never want to see Africa again." He had always been afraid that Orbius had suspected him, if he sailed he would never return.

"You are still able to climb this particularly steep hill." The words were a command and the look in the Roman's eyes reminded Dasius of his father. There had been times when Sextus Cornelius had refused to listen to entreaty or explanation.

"I cut the bushes, I led you along the coast. Let me live my last years here in peace."

"There is no danger, unless you are seasick. The ship is well armed, we shall give you funds and the captain will be instructed to give you all the help in his power. Besides with a fair wind you ought to be back at Neapolis in less than two months."

Kallistus would hide him but it would mean moving to another city and leaving his home. Then as if this thought had to link itself to a similar memory, the word home reminded him of Mago. Perhaps his friend was still there, waiting for him, sitting in front of the circular well where he had rubbed the ointment into the Roman's legs. He glanced down instinctively but they were covered by the toga, "I hope the thorns left no scars."

Orbius shrugged his shoulders. He would have preferred a skin pitted with marks to the fester in his mind. He looked at the trader; yes, there were a dozen younger men whom he could have sent on what was, for all his words, a dangerous voyage, but he could never forgive Dasius for having been happy in Africa. He was startled himself at the contempt in his voice as he said, "you may name your reward."

A tiny lizard ran along the wall. It was a lucky omen. "My reward?" A prison camp would not have broken his father as it seemed to have broken this man. "If I go, it will be for my city and not a bar of silver. I want Roman citizenship."

Orbius stared. He had been mistaken, the trader was as loyal as himself. He was tempted for a moment to send another man but Dasius should have his wish if it were possible. "The citizenship! It would have been easier if you had asked me for five gold staters but bring us the news and I will do all in my power to get it for you. My servant will come in the morning to fetch you to my house and there I will give you your instructions."

CHAPTER 17

The street was bare. If Dasius had been asked what changes he noticed after eight years of absence, he would have answered, "the emptiness and the dirt." It had been so clean formerly that the sailors had said jokingly they could eat a meal off the pavement and it had hardly been an exaggeration. The stalls had been divided from each other in the market place and the spaces in front of them continually swept. Now the stones looked as if nobody had touched them for a week, flies rose from the garbage piles at every corner and bits of plaster from the walls lay in the gutter. How was he to find anything to interest Orbius in this desolate, impoverished place? If he ventured away from the trading quarter he might be stabbed for the sake of the few obols that he carried for necessities in his bag.

People stared at him as he walked along although he had again taken the precaution of buying an unbelted, Carthaginian robe. Every other man he met was a Numidian. They stood in amazement in front of the still magnificent temples but otherwise pushed the citizens out of their way. An African with a blue bead necklace round his powerful throat elbowed him maliciously to the wall and he wished he were aboard the ship again. The three weeks that the captain intended to remain in port stretched interminably into the future.

Dasius strolled slowly along the quay because he wanted to find the inn where Mago and he had stayed on their infrequent visits to Carthage. It would be dangerous. The innkeeper might recognize him but he would have no peace until he knew what had happened to his friend. The place had been kept by a man they called the Sicilian although from his features he must have been born in Carthage but the appearance of the quarter had altered, he found what he thought was the house but stopped in time as he was about to enter it. It was full of officials. One of them stared at him suspiciously as he turned away and a circle of shouting urchins surrounded him, each anxious to take him to a different tavern. "Do you know the inn they call the Sicilian's?" he asked the cleanest boy in the group. He could not remember or perhaps had never heard the man's real name.

"That old place! I'll take you to Himilcon's, it's got a garden, it's new."

"No, I want to see the Sicilian, I've got a message for him." A look passed round the circle and the other boys slid away so swiftly that Dasius wondered if the inn had changed owners and had now got a bad reputation? He followed his guide through a mass of alleys into ever shabbier streets until the boy stopped finally in front of a little, dusty courtyard. He was about to protest that they had come to the wrong house when he saw the carving of a boat inside a shallow niche that had so amused Mago, "a puff of wind and that mast would break, it's set at a wrong angle."

"I'll wait for you to give the message and then take you back to Himilcon's. Only fishermen come here."

"No," Dasius gave the urchin a coin and dismissed him. He was not sure himself that he could find the way to the harbor again but his errand could not be hurried, it might take a couple of hours. An old man with gray hair came slowly towards him without a sign of recognition on his face.

"It's a long time since I was here," he must disguise the story slightly so as not to be linked with the Roman landing, "I came one spring ten years ago with a cargo from Greece."

"You will not find much in the city you remember."

"No, I had to take a guide to bring me here."

"I wonder he did not take you to Himilcon and the famous new garden? In my day, those places near the naval harbor were kept for officials."

"You used to serve a wonderful dish of mullet when I was here last."

"With the Alexandrian sauce?"

"Yes."

"Come in," the Sicilian led the way through a passage that was half full of empty baskets into a second court-yard behind the house. It was clean, the pavement had been washed that morning and was not quite dry while two fig trees, from the color of their trunks they must be very old, cast intricate shadows on the white wall behind them. "To think that you have remembered the mullet after all these years! I must see what I have. The fishermen still come to me but otherwise it's quiet. I'm in the wrong part of the city now for merchants."

"Have some wine with me and tell me the news. There are only strangers like myself where I am staying."

"A moment," the old man hurried away and Dasius could hear him shouting orders, no doubt to the slaves in the kitchen. He came back carrying a plate of figs and a jug and put them on the table himself. "Water with figs, as I'm sure you'll remember, we'll have wine later with the fish."

"Trade is poor," Dasius remembered that the Sicilian had seldom talked much to his guests and he wanted to win the man's confidence, "I sold a few bales the day after my arrival but nothing since."

"You should have been here before Hannibal was elected magistrate. They used to take more than half we earned away from us and one of my own neighbors died for want of a little food. I did what I could but you cannot help everybody. The Commander was just. Do you know," the old man struck the table in his fury, "he found that we could pay the tribute to Rome each year from what the officials had stolen themselves out of our tolls. And under him, the prices fell too, I was able to buy some new pots for the kitchen. Only his year of office finished in the spring and we are wondering now what will happen?"

"They say that the ruling families hate him."

"They cannot forgive him his victories."

Dasius began to eat a fig slowly, it was true that this fruit grew better in Africa although it was so liquid and so sweet that he would have thought it needed rain more than the incessant sunlight. The information that Orbius had given him was correct; there was a rift between the Carthaginian masses and their masters as violent as between two rival cities. The small shopkeepers, the returned soldiers and the sailors who had lost their vessels were ready to follow Hannibal if he lifted a finger but it was the landowners who had the power. They could cut off supplies of grain to the city as they had done before in its history and they could also hire Numidians to protect them. He wondered idly if that was why there were so many of them about the streets?

"You should have been here three years ago," the Sicilian continued, "the tolls were so high that a fisherman could not even sell his catch. But what do the magistrates care if the sailors starve?"

"Talking of sailors, can you tell me what happened to a Captain Mago? He first brought me here."

The Sicilian looked up suddenly at the trader's face. "Now I remember, you are the Greek who lived with him and disappeared when the Romans landed."

"I was trying to join him when I was taken prisoner. They sent me back to Italy because I was skilled with ciphers and there by chance a kinsman saw me and I was ransomed."

He made up a story quickly.

"I have been working for him at Neapolis ever since."

"Why have you come back here?"

"To find my friend."

"He lost his ship."

"But he still had the farm."

The Sicilian bit into a second fig as if he wanted time to think things over. Dasius longed to take him by the neck and shake him but he knew that he had to wait patiently until the old man was ready to talk. "If you had stayed at the farm as Mago told you," the innkeeper said finally, "you need never have left Africa."

The yells of "stone the spy" that he had heard while he had hidden shivering behind the lattice, rang in the trader's ears but he held his tongue and took a silver drachma out of his bag instead to slap on the table. "I am terrified of the sea but I risked the voyage here to find my friend."

The Sicilian looked greedily at the coin but did not touch it. "News for your Roman masters! Are they afraid of our captains even without their ships?"

"I am a Greek. I was taken prisoner. What is Rome to me?"

"Mago was one of our best navigators but he was not a wise man."

"What did he do?"

"He only said what all were muttering in the harbor, that if men and money had been sent to Hannibal in time, there would have been no invasion and we should have kept our ships but he had to shout this out in the middle of the square and his words were reported to the magistrates."

"And then what happened?"

"They would have sent him to the mines but there was such a turmoil among the sailors, that the judges fined him heavily instead and banished him from Carthage. He had to sell his property and he went eastward to some kinsmen. I have never seen him since."

"Is he still alive?"

"I do not know." He put his hand firmly over the silver as if to show that they had ended the discussion.

An elderly slave came forward with a dish and served them with the mullet. "The Alexandrian sauce!" the Sicilian said solemnly, taking the cover off a bowl. He helped himself plentifully as if it had been a long time since he had eaten a full meal. "And now, tell me about Neapolis," he continued, "is it free or are the Romans in control of the city? And do you pay many tolls?"

"Tell me who likes the tax collector?" Dasius pretended to be busy removing the bones from his fish because he wanted to avoid a political discussion. The food was clean but it was no better than in any little tavern outside Neapolis. The cooks, like everyone else in Carthage, had lost their art.

"Are you staying long?"

"The captain wants to sail as soon as his ship is loaded but that will not be for another ten days. Meantime may I have another helping of your excellent sauce?" He did not want it but he knew that it would flatter the Sicilian.

"Do you think it needs a dash more pepper? I am elderly and like it mild but you . . ."

"It could not be bettered."

How different it was to the days when he had rushed here from the market to meet Mago and tell him about the man on his way to the temple with a lion cub in his basket or the rogue who had stuffed a bag of olives inside the cone of his hat. "You are like a boy," the sailor would say, shaking his head, yet it had been Mago who had declared that there could not be an invasion because the Roman captains would be afraid to go so far from land. He listened now to the innkeeper but without giving him his full attention while the man grumbled about the poverty, the prices and what he called the insolence of the new Carthaginians, men who had enriched themselves during the difficult years after the invasion. Dasius nodded and asked, at the first convenient pause, "and now what do I owe you for the meal? I have a merchant coming to look at one of my bales and I must not be late."

The Sicilian's face brightened, he had evidently thought the fish was to be included in the silver drachma. He named a price greedily that was as much as the famous Himilcon would have charged but Dasius paid it without protest.

"You will come again? I could get you some young tunny fish or would you prefer some meat?"

"I leave myself in your hands. I will come the day after tomorrow and bring you one of my wine cups if you will get me the name of Mago's kinsman and of the village. They are real Samian and the official who saw me at my entry bought three for his own household."

"What use is a Samian cup to me?" the old man said bitterly, looking at a loose stone in the pavement.

"Then let it be another coin although your tolls are double what I pay at Neapolis." Dasius had already noticed with concern that he had spent as much in a week as he had expected would last him for three and that soon he would have nothing left to buy goods to fill his bales for the return. The simplest dish was double what it would have cost him in Italy.

"It's so long ago, nobody will remember him."

"Try, his sailors will if you can find one." The old man looked anxious but Dasius put his bag ostentatiously inside his robe. "The fish I leave to you, it could not be better than today." He knew that it was less avarice with the Sicilian than genuine poverty and age.

"You can trust me." In answer to a shout, a ragged

boy came out of the kitchen and held open the door. "He will take you back to where you are staying, you may get lost otherwise among these winding streets." The Sicilian hesitated a moment, he prodded the loose stone with the tip of his sandal and then he added in a low voice, "Be careful, do not go out at night, many people I know have disappeared."

It was growing dark but Dasius could still see the bay in front of him where Mago had chosen to end what had become a useless life. "He jumped into the sea from that rock there," his kinsman had said, "a boy saw him and we pulled him out but it was too late."

His friend's death troubled the trader's own newly won peace because whatever Kallistus had said to him about wisdom was relative, it was not true for a man who had lost the chance to do the work for which he had been superbly trained. "You are wrong, Kallistus," Dasius muttered, walking up and down the road along the edge of the shore, "it is easier for a fool to be contented than a thinker." His own past came back to him as he moved, sometimes the memories were shadowy, sometimes they revolved in their bright, original colors, he saw the Carthaginian camp in the hills and a man rubbing a silver lion's head on a shield as if he were still standing in front of him although why it should return to him at this moment when he had not even spoken to the soldier, he could not say. There had been two supremely happy moments in his life, the childhood at Tarentum, his two years with Mago. Both had been instantly destroyed by forces over which he had had no control. "He could not forget that he was a captain," a fisherman had said harshly earlier that day. They did not understand, it was not the power that Mago had missed but the opportunity to use his skill. Banishment had subjected him to a premature aging while his body was still powerful and comparatively young. Perhaps this was the flaw in the Carthaginian character? They could not yield. They considered themselves bound by immutable laws and could not adapt themselves if catastrophes occurred. Yes, in spite of Mago's reproaches, it was his own native restlessness, Dasius knew, that had kept him alive.

The village was about twenty miles east of Carthage but it had taken him a day and a half to reach it on the back of a hired and awkward mule. It was a fishing settlement and he had found Mago's kinsman without much difficulty and had even felt that the man was glad to see him. He had feared that they might have been suspicious of his foreign accent but they had assumed at once that he had been born in Carthage but among the families of mixed races around the harbor. "He left nothing," they had told him at once, "and we sold his clothes to pay for the burial. Perhaps it was for the best," one of the men added, "he was drinking a lot at the end and sometimes then he said dangerous things about our rulers. It was a pity he had to leave his own home. I think he was lonely here."

Dasius stared out to sea but night had come, it was merely a surface of small, dark waves. If he had come back earlier, could he have rescued Mago? It was honesty, and not for the sake of his own peace, if the answer was no. A Greek stranger could have found no work in the village and the only way that he could have taken Mago to Neapolis was as a slave. Fate had separated them as mercilessly as the few days at sea had cut him from his birthplace to throw him into the formless misery of his years with Alfius and all that a man could do was to bear his lot with courage. "No," he shouted although there was only a seagull or two to hear him, there must be another way, he resented such helplessness with all the energy that he possessed. "Oh, Mago, Mago, if you could only know that I came back to find you!" The peasants would think him mad and start pelting him with stones if they heard him muttering aloud. The stars, the very stars that he had watched so often with his friend, went on shining tranquilly in the almost black sky as they had shone on the dying in the gardens of sacked cities or the ship that had foundered on a rock, immune from fear or rage or did they, Dasius wondered fancifully, have their own trials, their own unknown motions of change?

He must return to the inn even if he could not sleep because he was to join a party at dawn returning to Carthage. His only consolation was the thought of his home at Neapolis. The presence of Kallistus might help him, if not the philosopher's words. He walked slowly back to the road, the evening had taken away the scent from the young bean flowers that had been so fragrant at noon, he kept his eyes on the sand to avoid looking again into the sky. He stopped, what were those hoof beats on the road behind him? Had some official found out who he was and sent soldiers to arrest him? "Roman spy!" He was no spy but how could he make them believe him? He crouched behind an outhouse, his queries and his resolution wiped out by terror, waiting for the men to halt.

The riders passed. One man was several lengths ahead of his companions. A short cloak flew behind his shoulders so that Dasius could see the familiar breastplate although it was too dark to separate the central emblem from the pattern of figures. He wore no helmet but reined his horse back a little and turned his head as if he were trying to fix the outline of the bay upon his mind. He did not stop completely but galloped forward after a moment, followed by his escort. There must be a ship waiting somewhere; if only Mago could have been its captain.

So Rome had won! Dasius had often said the words but this was the first time that his heart recognized their truth. Perhaps only a Greek could understand what it meant to a man to lose his city? The veterans, the sailors, simple people like the Sicilian would survive no more than Mago. It was the end of an age.

He ran into the road. The horsemen were rounding the corner. All that the Greek could think of was the army proverb. "In every pair one of the swordsmen is defeated, no matter who wins the battle. It's a man's friends who matter at the finish." Now Hannibal was gone and Mago was dead.

CHAPTER 18

"You must leave at once, Dasius," the Sicilian said uneasily, "listen to that noise. They will call out the Guard."

The street in front of them was empty but an angry roar was rising from the neighboring wharf and there was a continual clatter of sandals as men ran down the hill to join the crowd. "You are right. The ship is sailing tomorrow and I don't want to get caught in some demonstration and detained."

"I shall remember you whenever I wear the cloak."

"It will keep you warm, I hope, on winter nights." Dasius had bought two lion skins with the remainder of the money that Orbius had given him, they would be an excuse for his journey and should fetch good prices at Neapolis, but he had hurried along that morning to take whatever he could spare from his own possessions to the old innkeeper and to tell him the result of his journey. "It was only with your help that I was able to find out what had happened to the captain."

"Mago is luckier than we are. He did not live to see Carthaginians betraying their leader in his own city to Rome."

"Not all Romans will be proud of what has happened."

"If only I could offer you some fish . . ." the old man glanced round the courtyard that he had prudently not repaired.

"I can't say some other time because the shouting is coming nearer and once I get to my inn, I shall stay there till I leave. No, don't send your boy with me, he might never get back and I know the way by now."

"Be sure to take the alley to your right just before you come to the cross roads. It's a bit further but that way you avoid the port."

"Bar your door and keep inside the house. I shall think of you when I get back to my garden at Neapolis."

"If it's the last time that I dare say the words aloud, Hannibal knew how we were wronged and fought the officials for us."

"At least he is out of their power. And now farewell, live in peace." Dasius lifted his hand in a final greeting and then hurried up the road, hoping that the old man's dwelling would look too humble for the Guard to molest him. It was a poor quarter of the city, there was a clutter of fish bones floating in a pool of dirty water in the gutter, all doors were shut, there was a pile of refuse against a wall. He hurried until he reached the turning that would have taken him to the upper town but there, instead of running so that he got out of the danger zone as rapidly as possible, he crossed to the opposite side of the road and walked down some narrow steps that led to the shore.

Dasius dared not go as far as the wharf itself. He had no wish to be wedged into the middle of a dangerous crowd where he might be taken for an official on account of his clothing and beaten. There was a patch of sunlight in front of him, he climbed a low wall that divided two houses from each other and found a stone where he could stand and look down at the harbor. There were only fishing vessels moored there now instead of merchant ships.

The quay was packed with a thick and angry mass; former sailors, veterans, peddlers and small craftsmen. To his surprise, there were even Numidians among them. "He paid the tribute," they stamped and chanted, "he paid the tribute from what the tax collectors had hidden in their households."

"What do the magistrates know of the cold at sea when we lose the shoal and come ashore with empty nets?"

"You charge enough for your fish when you catch it!" Dasius recognized the speaker. He had come once or twice to the Sicilian's table for his supper.

"They take half of all I earn and until Hannibal came, how much went to the Treasury and how much to some official's cellar?"

"I fought at Trebia and what did I get for it? Scars and fever."

"And the right to beg at the entrance to the market."

"They have arrested his bodyguard."

"No, not all, some of the men got away."

"To die in the sands?"

"No, to beg at Utica." Even Dasius joined in the laughter, it was the neighbor and rival of Carthage but even more friendly to Rome.

"Hannibal! Hannibal!" It was a roar as if the temple lions had broken from their chains.

"They have seized his estates."

"But he will come back with an army and conquer them."

If he only could, Dasius thought, but he knew that it was impossible. Even if the Commander had been able to take his gold with him, it would hardly suffice for a bodyguard, it could not hire an army. There was little chance that Hannibal would ever see Carthage again. Perhaps it was the lesson of this turbulent age? The survivors were those who could move with altered circumstances instead of being so rooted to their customs and their houses that they were easily destroyed.

"Follow me!" A huge Ethiopian bellowed from the top of the crowd. "Follow me!" We will burn the palaces and the traitors who live in them."

"And the Guard?"

"There are more of us."

"What have we to lose?"

It was the hush that Mago had taught him to expect before a tornado. The people were silent. Then they surged forward behind the Ethiopian and somebody dashed out with a torch from a house.

"Run!" A voice yelled from a roof top. "Run! It's too late."

The Guard came towards the quay, helmets on their heads, their shields well in front of them, swords in their hands.

"Run!" There were yells from every side but the men were wedged together and only a few individuals at the edges could break away. The Guard stopped. A trumpet sounded. A volley of sling shots crashed into the crowd. Some jumped in panic into the water, others were cut down by the swordsmen as they crouched on the ground.

Dasius watched, unable to move. The body of the veteran from Trebia lay doubled over on the pavement. A slinger strolled to the edge of the quay and as the swimmers tried to grasp a rope dangling from some boat to haul themselves out of the sea, he aimed at their hands. Some of the Guard turned and began to search the houses. The man whom he had seen at the Sicilian's dashed past him in terror, a gash from a stone across the side of his head. The sight seemed to release the trader's legs, he turned and followed him, up and up, racing in and out of a maze of passages until he came into the safety of an open square in front of a temple.

There was just enough movement for the ship to glide over waves that seemed to be of her own making. The oars were shipped, the wind filled the sail. Dasius noticed as he woke that he must have slept away the afternoon. He stretched, got to his feet and walked to the side to watch the foam dissolving at the bow. The captain had feared that morning that the breeze might drop but it had held; in two days if the weather did not break, they would enter the harbor of Neapolis.

Now that he was so near home, he was grateful to Orbius. The Roman had done him, without knowing it, a great service. This journey had uprooted his longing for Africa. The years with Mago would always be a band of color across his mind, they had come late in terms of age but they, rather than the lonely days at

Formiae, had been adventure and youth. So many other things had fallen into place and increased his impatience to get ashore. First he must report to Orbius. The tribune might have heard already about Hannibal's flight but he, Dasius, had actually witnessed it and as he had no idea of the port to which the Carthaginian leader was bound, the account could not harm him. The sight of the slinger killing the terrified fishermen as if they were rats, had disgusted him so much that he felt no scruples over giving Orbius whatever news he had collected. Carthage had taxed its population to such an extent that corruption was a necessity and they had driven out the only man who, once again, might have saved them.

It was a lonely voyage and Dasius longed to be ashore. The captain had indicated to him where he could eat and sleep but had otherwise ignored him. When he got home the second crop of roses would be opening in his garden, the buds the identical white of the waterlilies in the narrow stone basin beside the trees and, if there were any sudden movements, it would only be the lizards sunning themselves on the wall. Once Kallistus had joined him and they were sitting on the bench to finish the conversation that Orbius had interrupted in the spring, he could say that his search had ended. He glanced down at the sea, the surface was like life itself, assured and beautiful, but who could guess what was happening in the depths? What motive had driven two great cities into conflict when there was room for them both? Sicily and Iberia had been plundered, the riches of Campania were lost. What was its countryside but a mass of weed grown fields and blackened walls where the soldiers, of both armies, had fired the farms? A man could ride across it for two days without seeing even a shepherd and his dog. Hannibal had begun to re-build Carthage and exile was his reward. How could Kallistus with his gentleness explain such facts or why Mago with his honesty had had to die whereas Orbius, with his bitter distrust of man or woman, had power and lived? Yet there were many races, many religions, at Neapolis and there, he owed this entirely to Kallistus, whether Orbius gave him the citizenship or not, he could reconcile the worlds of his Greek mother and his Roman father, and be at peace.

The lookout yelled. There was a scuffle as the sleepy rowers scrambled back to their benches, several sailors ran along the deck. "Roll up your bedding and go below," an officer shouted as he hurried to the steersman's side.

"Is it a squall?" Dasius looked up but the sea was as placid as the sky.

"A squall? Call it that if you like. Haven't you seen the ship? He pointed to a vessel approaching them from the shore. It had the slim lines of a raider and a double bank of oars.

"I am a good swordsman," Dasius said quietly, aware that the officer was watching his face to see if it changed color.

"We have eight soldiers aboard and two bowmen. Besides, if the wind freshens we may slip away from them. It's rare to see raiders so far up the coast."

"I'm not a soldier but I have fought before, only I have no weapon."

"Stow your bedding, wait below, and if they board, we'll find you a dagger."

Dasius was not afraid but his hands shook with anger

as he pushed his belongings into a corner of the hold where they would not be in the way and sat down on top of them. He was tired of danger, the dream was broken and, superstitiously, he tried not to think of Neapolis. He had never been in a fight at sea but he had mixed so much with sailors that he knew what would happen. First a challenge, then a shower of arrows, finally the thud of sandals as the raiders jumped onto the deck. "If only the wind would get up," a soldier said, looking no more eager to fight than Dasius as he slipped the linen cover from his heavy shield.

"Where have they come from? There's no anchorage here."

"There's a bay and they hide in it, perhaps only for a few hours. What are the villagers to do? If they provide them with supplies, the pirates leave them alone. If they try to warn the next town, the stronger men are taken as slaves and the rest are killed. They probably think we come from Sicily, they'll have a surprise when our bowmen shoot."

It was hard to wait in the semi-darkness under the poop. The rowers swung backwards and forwards, trying to gain a little speed. Dasius could hear their heavy breathing and smell their sweat. A cockroach dropped from a beam and he stamped on it with disgust. Why had he had to spend so much of his life in filth when he so loved white linen and clean air? What use were the speculations of Kallistus to him now? The world split into two halves exactly like a pomegranate with the thinkers one side and the doers on the other. At the end it was force that won. If the raiders boarded, they would be killed or enslaved unless, but of this he was doubtful, the soldiers could beat them off. He would

226

be at a disadvantage with a short dagger against a man with a sword. He was tired, it was less a physical condition than some complete exhaustion of the mind, one danger had led to another until he could only feel an immense irritation and fatigue. This new peril was unfair, it re-awakened his grief for Mago, he wanted somebody near him to whom he could talk. The stink, the pitching of the vessel made him dizzy and if he vomited here, they would think he was afraid. He grabbed a bolt or clung to the side until he reached the officer who was assembling his men. "This motion is worse than waiting to be boarded, give me the dagger and let me come with you on deck."

"Keep your head down then, you have no shield."

It was good to be in the fresh air as he followed them to the stern. The raider was creeping up rapidly, he could see its sailors loosening a rope. There was a hail but nobody caught the exact words. A javelin crashed into the screen around the steersman but without doing him any harm. Two soldiers moved towards him to protect him and the archers crawled to the bow. A series of incongruous images raced through the trader's mind as he lay flat on the deck, clinging to a bar. He was striding towards a Carthaginian outpost where a friend of his was making pancakes from stolen eggs, Kallistus was stepping hurriedly aside from a wet roll of leaves that had looked exactly like a frog, he was trying to keep awake inside a smoky inn. . . . "Ah," the crew yelled, an arrow had struck the raider's steersman and his comrades were dragging him away. "I should never have thought that an arrow would have carried that distance," the sailor next to him muttered.

The raider seemed to hesitate, she was a beautiful

sight as the wind filled her linen sail, "she's turning," the captain shouted, "they did not know we were armed." In another moment both ships would be out of bow-shot. The sky darkened, the wind increased, they began to pitch violently, at the top of the roll Dasius could see the vessel drawing away, then, the next moment, they, themselves, seemed level with the water. A wave broke over them and, forgetting the danger, he struggled instinctively to his knees and clutched the rail. "Down, you fool," the sailor yelled but it was too late. A final javelin hurtled through the air straight at the Greek's chest.

"What do you want done with this?" the officer asked, half an hour later, pointing to the body. They had shipped the oars, the ship was rolling evenly and the raider was a mere line on the horizon.

"Search him and throw him to the dolphins. If the fool had obeyed his orders and stayed below, he would still be alive."

"I hope it won't mean trouble at Neapolis. He was on an errand for one of the tribunes."

"They should have sent a warship to clear the coast instead of trying to find excuses to keep the fleet in harbor. I was frightened, I can tell you, when I saw that raider gaining on us."

"They would have boarded us if we had not hit their steersman."

"It was a magnificent shot, the man should be rewarded."

The officer nodded, he did not like being on a merchantman. It was hard to fight properly on the rolling deck of a damaged ship that might sink during the

combat but what else could he do? The transport fleet
had been dispersed after the war and, having no influ-
ence, he had had to take the only post that had been
offered to him. Nobody liked to pull a dart out of a corpse
and he could leave that to one of his soldiers but as he
stooped down to see if the trader had carried a money
bag under his belt, what struck him most was a huge
squashed cockroach on the sole of the Greek's sandal.

"Here's a bag but there are only a couple of coins in
it."

"He had some bales stowed among the cargo."

"He asked me for a weapon and I thought at the time
they would board us in force."

"Get him overboard, I don't want to go on looking
at him but warn the men that all his goods must be
delivered to the tribune or they may get beaten. Still, if
you can find that cloak he wore, you can bring it to me.
It was mountain wool from Apulia and my own is stiff
with salt."

CHAPTER 19

The great gold plain that was sheltered by a line of hills stretched below the terrace of the Tibur inn. Zonas could not see the Forum from his seat but only the confused lines of many buildings and an occasional arch. Rome was there, the reality behind the name that had accompanied his life, terrifying or assisting him, according to circumstances. A light dust hid part of the city, it could not choke him here as it might have done if he had been driving a mule through the streets, it was simply an apricot colored haze in the evening sky. "Times change." How often he had heard the phrase shouted about the taverns but suddenly it was true. Now the only danger on the roads was meeting some huge wagon in charge of an aggressive freedman, taking the household goods of some wealthy family from their country villa back to the city when the hot weather was over. To his surprise, it was Melania whom he missed the most; more than Sikelia, almost more than his youth. It must be five years now since he had found the donkey dead in her stall but the gods had only taken his wife the previous summer, as swiftly as if they had wantonly shot an arrow at her, as she was bustling up the hill on a hot afternoon. He would not pray the Messenger to wait for him. His idleness fretted him and all the things that were beyond his strength. Only a year ago he had joined his companions in the big tavern at the end of the market place but this autumn his body was as worn out as Sikelia's had been, the months before she died. "Patience, Lucius," he said, looking down at a small boy who was playing noisily at his feet, "your master will be here in a moment to say farewell and afterwards we will have supper."

He was tired but not hungry, not at least for the sort of food that was all he could eat at present. What had happened to Dasius? He had watched for him during several springs. If the Greek had not wandered into that wretched village in the mountains, how long was it ago, almost a man's lifetime, he would not be sitting here with land and oxen of his own, respected by all his neighbors. Life had been rich while Melania was alive but nothing seemed to matter any more. "Let me go . . . let me go . . ." he muttered aloud in a sort of prayer and Lucius, seeing that no one was watching him, stole away to the exciting stalls on the neighboring road.

"Drowsy, Zonas? What good wine have your friends been serving you?"

Zonas started. He thought as he opened his eyes that Karus, alone of them all, had kept something of youth. His hair was still dark, his movements confident and light, and he stood there, smiling at the old man, scarcely heavier than when he had ridden home on Sikelia's back more than twenty years previously.

"I am old," Zonas answered, it was a statement, not a complaint, "this is my last market."

"You've been saying that for years, yet you always spend the summer fattening up the sheep so as to come here again and bargain." Yet Karus knew as he looked at the sunken cheeks with the white wrinkles under the sunburnt skin that Zonas was right and that it was probably the last time he would ever see him. The winter sickness was hard on the old. "I hope Lucius has not been tiring you? The steward will take charge of him as soon as the market is over."

"Lucius! Where is the child?" He looked round guiltily but the boy had seen Karus coming and had followed him down the steps. "He wants his supper as all boys do but it is good for him to learn patience."

"Oh, he needs discipline, that's why I'm leaving him at the farm. Rome in winter is a cold place for either a puppy or a child. There's nowhere for them to run."

"We will do what we can."

"Here, Lucius, go and buy yourself a cake." The boy was staring at them insolently; he took the coin that Karus gave him and went back towards the stalls without a word of thanks.

It had been foolish to buy him, Karus admitted constantly, but when he had seen a man beating the child, the contrast between the boy's gray eyes and sharp, Punic nostrils had awakened his pity. "It's a long time since the fighting stopped and I cannot go on hating helpless people," he said apologetically, knowing that Zonas would agree with him.

"His father was a Carthaginian hostage?"

"Yes, he is said to have escaped into the hills. I suppose with those eyes, the mother must have been a slave from some tribe in the north?"

"You will have trouble with him. He has the African moodiness and too much pride." They had been unwise, Zonas thought, to give the child a Roman name. It was going to be as hard for him when he grew up as it had been for Dasius and he had been free born. Perhaps the Greek had found a place for himself in some distant city where nobody had known about Alfius or his youth?

It was the last moment of dusk; the sunset, it was like a general's cloak, was turning from scarlet into a gray that matched the Tibur walls. Karus looked across the plain that was still a hazy gold. He was among the things he loved, Rome, the sea and the hills. After the war, unlike most of the survivors, he had found his place. Fortune had given him two gifts; some wisdom and his city, from the arches of the temples to the chariot ruts in the roads outside the gates.

Lucius came back, his face half buried in his cake and suddenly as he looked at the boy's now happy eyes, Karus remembered Verna. She too had been half a Gaul. It must have been years since he had thought of her but now that he had been initiated into the mysteries, unlike the country people, he did not believe that she would be forever in the shades. Perhaps she was part of that wind that was beginning to rise among the mountains? He wished now that he had freed her before he had left but he had been afraid of his mother's anger. He had learned in the intervening years that to try not to hurt some person might involve several others in disaster. His mother even might have lived to see him return from Africa if she had had Verna as her companion. Oh, why did one only learn years afterwards the right way to have avoided some fault?

"Was it good?" he asked as Lucius licked a last crumb from his mouth. The boy nodded and Karus handed him a second small coin, "you may buy another when you have your supper. There is only one big market every year."

There was water trickling into a shallow basin and a small heap of dead leaves at the side of the path. Several women with baskets on their heads and a man leading a brown mule with a white patch on its leg walked slowly down the road. "Your son sold the sheep-skins for more than they were worth but I could hardly persuade him to have a cup of wine with me afterwards." Zonas was worth both his children, Karus thought, and for a moment, he saw, not Tibur but the hut in the valley where the trader had nursed him in spite of the hills round them being full of the enemy.

"Melania won. She kept both of my sons from the road." It had been his one great disappointment.

"But not from the sea." The trader's second boy was a carpenter and therefore half way to an officer, on a warship stationed at Ostia.

"And what was strange, he took Mocco's son with him."

"Poor Mocco! He had other children but he never understood his boy leaving a good farm for storms and dangers."

"We can't always keep a mule on the path and a man

has to follow his will," Zonas grumbled, "it was the sacrifice this morning that made me drowsy, I can't drink anything without falling asleep."

Karus stood watching the old man, wondering what to say. These meetings with the elderly were so difficult. "It's the same with my friend, Orbius. Do you remember what a magnificent horseman he was? Yet now he has to take a stick if he walks across the atrium."

Much as Karus hated to admit it, even to himself, they had nothing now to say to each other. He dreaded the visits when he sat in the smoke of several braziers in an overheated room, trying to talk with long pauses between sentences and no interests in common and each of them longing secretly for the afternoon to be over.

"He was a prisoner for years. A man always suffers from such an experience."

"A Greek called Dasius helped him to escape. It couldn't have been your friend, it was a merchant who was captured while sailing to Sicily. Of course, it's a common name."

"No," Zonas shook his head, "but do you know, just before you came I was wondering what had happened to the fellow?"

"He must be dead or he would have come to see you again. Orbius heard that the man he knew was killed during another voyage."

"It is wrong to tempt Fortune too often."

"Take anything of mine you want during the winter, Zonas. Are they looking after you now that your wife has died?"

"They give me all I need." It was true that now that they were useless to him, he could have everything he wanted, wine, meat, fleeces, even a girl.

"I have never forgotten that you saved my life." How hard it was to express gratitude and yet how often he remembered the trader helping him gently onto Sikelia's back, if he jumped into running water on a hot day or walked up the orchard in the evening. "Be sure to take Melania's remedy if you have a cough. Whatever was the stuff?"

"Fumitory," Zonas wrinkled his face up in a grimace. "I'm awake now, send Lucius to me and may Fortune be with you." It was the greeting of the market place and they both smiled.

"Farewell," Karus hesitated a moment but there were experiences that could not be expressed in words. "I shall ride out to see you as soon as the snows are over, meantime, be happy, keep well."

"You'll wear out that sheath if you keep playing with it," Zonas scolded. Karus had bought the child a tiny knife shaped like a dagger in the market.

"When do we have dinner?" the boy answered sulkily.

"As soon as the steward comes."

"You said we should have it at once."

It was natural for a child to be impatient. The day that Domina Sybilla had appointed him to the farm seemed less important now to Zonas than that evening in his childhood when a sailor had pushed away his half filled bowl and he had had a whole mullet to himself for the first time in his life. He remembered the sting of the sauce and how he had licked his fingers after finishing it. "When I went to Ostia to see my son . . ."

"You've told me that before," Lucius said cruelly, "I'm hungry."

It had been the trader's final expedition but although

it had given him "a breath of new life" to smell the nets and see the fish again, Ostia was not Formiae. He had lost himself entering the dockyard and though the crew of his son's ship had been friendly, they were strangers. He wondered sleepily why he had never re-visited his birthplace? Karus had offered him the time but one year a bridge had been carried away in a flood, another spring there had been sickness among the flocks and after his elder son had learned enough to take over some of the responsibilities, he had felt too old to take the journey. The sulky child beside him slashed at a leaf. He had obviously been ill treated before Karus had bought him and flew into a rage if people noticed his Punic features. "If you try breaking in a puppy too soon, it will never make a watch dog," Zonas quoted when they discussed some new outburst in the kitchen. Fortunately the boy was in the steward's charge and he had little to do with him. "What's that?" There were shouts from one end of the market place to the other and the noise of people running out of the booths. Lucius sprang up and would have gone to join them if Zonas had not grasped him by the arm.

He had once seen a blaze among the stalls and the faces looking afterwards at the ashes of the goods that should have bought their winter food. "Wait!" Lucius was tugging like an angry puppy to get away from his grasp, "we will go together to see what has happened." He reached for his stick, hesitated before he began to climb the steep, narrow steps and as he put his foot on the bottom one, he saw Karus come running towards them again, his cloak flying in an undignified manner behind his shoulders. "It's Hannibal," he shouted as soon as he was within earshot, "it's Hannibal, he's dead."

"Dead?" It was long ago in time but every detail of the face, every inflection of the voice, was clearer to Zonas than the great stone slab immediately in front of his eyes.

"A company of soldiers surrounded the house. He saw them and took poison. It's true, the tribune at Tibur told me himself."

"In Bithynia?"

"In Bithynia."

"He's dead, he's dead," Lucius clapped his hands, "our enemy is dead."

"Silence," Karus roared, there was something of a cunning, angry elephant in the child's broad face, "respect the fallen."

"But he was our enemy."

"He was your leader."

"My leader! I'm Roman. I'm glad he died."

"That's because you never saw him."

Zonas sat down on the bench again. He wished that the steward would come and take the child away. Hannibal! He must have been a year or two older than himself, too old to lift a shield, yet Rome had grudged the season or two left to him and the chance to die quietly with his memories in his own room. Words floated down from the groups above them, "my grandfather was killed at Trebia," that must be the saddler from the shop beside the inn, "I was at Zama" and a strange voice, "that time the sling shot hit me at Tarentum, I never thought I would see Tibur again." All the people were quiet, they were remembering their past experiences soberly and without anger. Then a yell burst above them all, "vengeance, vengeance, Rome has taken vengeance" and a band of youths began to stamp as they shouted. What did those children know of sling shots or forced marches? What did they know of life? Dame Sybilla, Dasius, Melania, his donkey, all had gone and he had outlived his usefulness. Nothing was left but the face on the money, a piece of dead silver. He fumbled with the old familiar gesture until he drew the leather bag from his coat, opened it and held the coin up for the last time in front of his tired eyes. The light caught it as if it were morning, he heard the voice saying again, "give the man his donkey and let him go," he saw the great shield. "I want you to take this," he held it out to Karus on the flat of his palm, "it was the means of my finding you that day."

"I cannot accept it," Karus knew how much it meant to the old man.

"I want you to have it." It was not true because Zonas would have liked to hold it in his fingers until he died. It was a symbol of victory, of the fact that in this harsh, uncertain world, some men shone above their fellows not through power but through understanding. Then he remembered that his son would exchange it at once for a meadow or a yoke of oxen and who knew into what hands it might fall? He pushed it firmly into his friend's hand.

"I will put it in my chest till the spring."

"No, I want you to have it, you have never said a word against him. Above all, do not give it to my son, it's worth more than a corn field."

How little one knew about one's fellow men, Karus thought, holding the coin up in his turn to look at the head. He had always considered Zonas to be an honest but sometimes crafty trader, rough in his life and feelings and always thinking about a bargain, yet it was he, in all the throng, who was the mourner at this day's news. "I will send a messenger out if I hear more in Rome, meantime, farewell until the spring." They both knew that there would be no meeting then but what else, Karus wondered, could he say?

Zonas nodded, he was drowsy again and he looked across the plain as if it were possible to see his son's too distant port. There was always the road, the road that the Carthaginian had just followed into freedom and that he would take himself before the snows. "It's been a long day," he said as if to excuse his sleepiness and then in a final outburst as he thought of the brutes who had refused to let an old man die in peace, he shouted so angrily that Lucius cowered under the bench behind him, "the stinking rats! O Hermes strike them! What pity, what pity is there ever for the vanquished?"